# The Son of the STREETS...

## A Novel
## By

## Terrence LeRoy Baker

## An
## Incarcerated Minds
## Production

## The Son of the Streets...
### Terrence leRoy Baker

Published By: Incarcerated Minds Production Corp. (USA)
Incarcerated Minds Production
1708 Adams, South Bend, IN 46628

Library of Congress Control Number: 2008925597
ISBN-13: 978-0-9816843-1-4
ISBN-10: 0-9816843-1-9

Front Cover Designed: Antwan "Hot Rod" McClay
Edited By: Crystal Baker
Photo of Author: Marc Weiss

Manufactured in the United States of America

For information regarding special discounts for bulk purchases, submitting titles, music, and movies for publishing please contact the Incarcerated Minds Production Corp. at 310-691-3553, e-mail: incarceratedminds@live.com

For reviews: www.myspace.com/terrencebaker
www.bookclubofamerica.ning.com

*The Son of the Streets...*
*Terrence leRoy Baker*

*This book is dedicated to my beautiful wife Crystal Baker who inspires me to be great, and to my lovely children.*

# **Introduction**

It all started back in about 1987. My mother always did the best she could to raise three children alone, but that wasn't easy considering the fact that two of us were boys. My older brother Romelo and I had the same no good father, and instead of spending quality time with him we would stay with his parents in his place. Our little sister Tawana had a different father, but still the same ol song. Life was hard growing up in the 1980's, but my grandparents did everything that they possibly could to ease that pain. They would accept my little sister into their home just like she was their grandchild.

Romelo and I also had another little sister on my father's side of the family, her name was Renea, and Renea and I was the exact same age. Go figure! My father was a busy man in the late 1970's and early 1980's. My grandparents had full custody of Renea, so whenever we visited she was there. But as you can see, my brother and I were inseparable. I looked up to my brother for everything; he was two years older than me and got all of the attention. I wanted to be just like him. My name is Terry, but everybody calls me Tea.

My father ran the streets, but in a spoiled kind of way. He would always depend on his parents to bail him out of the tight jams that he would constantly end up in. I can count on one hand the amount of times I spent with that man, and of those, maybe one or two were pleasant. So as expected, my grandfather was always the father figure in my life: the image. But as we all know the image is only as good as your imagination, and I didn't have a very good one.

My grandfather was a strong hard working man from the south. He came up to Indiana as a young boy, and found his way on his own. I loved him for being such a good man, and he was great at keeping out of opinion based thinking. Whenever my grandmother or anybody else would speak rumor, he would ease out of the conversation just far enough to support his wife and keep his distance. I always thought of the Cosby's when I looked at my grandparents.

Our grandparents taught us everything about manners and respect. If it weren't for their presence in our lives, I seriously doubt I would've lived long enough to tell this story. "The Story of my Life"

## <u>Chapter 1</u>

I remember it like it was just yesterday. My father had gotten his girlfriend from Michigan pregnant and announced that they were to get married.

"You children need to find you someone you love, and get married before you decide to go around having babies," my grandmother told us all very sternly. I will always remember that day because of those words. Young as I was they made so much sense.

That Sunday was different from any other. I went to Sunday school on a mission to find me a wife. I was even excited about going to church, and as you know, most children are not. That day was the day that I was going to find my wife, and sure enough: I did.

I was only seven years old and could swear to you; it was love at first sight. Our class was held in the Red room at the Macedonian Church basement. We both had grown up going to church together, but this was the first time I ever recognized her. I still can remember that curly hair all over her head and those beautiful chubby cheeks. I was mesmerized by such beauty, as I held her gaze, I wondered if God could ever make anything so perfect and real for me.

Nothing else in that room mattered any more; I probably stared at her for the whole time. She had to know that I was looking at her because it was as if we were speaking the language of love without words. As I sat there flabbergasted and wondering who was this angel sent to me from God himself, the teacher interrupted my thoughts and said "Charity, please introduce yourself to the class."

That was it 'Charity', the name of my future wife. What a beautiful name to match such a beautiful person, I thought.

"Hi," I said to my first love after the class was over. "My name is Terry"

"Hi," She said back to me with a cute little blush on her face. "How old are you?"

"I am seven about to turn eight. How old are you?" I asked.

"I am six about to turn seven."

"So, will you marry me?" I asked making a complete fool out of myself.

"Boy you are crazy!" Charity said laughing at me in my face. "You are cute though"

"Thank you, so are you."

"Bye, Bye, Terry," she told me as she gave me a peck on my cheek.

"Bye!" I said, vowing to never wash my face again.

On the ride home from church that evening I told my grandmother, "Granny, you don't have to worry about me anymore, I've found my wife." She looked back at me from the passenger seat of their brand new Cadillac, "Boy what are you talking about?"

Defensively I told her everything that happened in Sunday school leaving out the most important part: my kiss. She just started laughing at me already knowing what little girl I was referring to. My grandfather was the only person in the car that wasn't laughing at me, but with me when he said, "Well you can't blame him, because we love our pretty women." My grandmother started to blush at his comment making everybody in the car laugh. I was serious though, and knew that one day I would show them all that the joke was never on me.

## Chapter 2

I grew up in a city by the name of South Bend Indiana. South Bend Indiana is a small city of size, but none the less a city full of big dreams. Growing up in South Bend was everything but easy.

As a young boy I always seemed to get involved with the wrong type of crowd. I don't know if it was my own personality or curiosity, but I was always the one asking questions; questions that the average kid my age didn't know the answers to. So, I had to lean on the older guys around the neighborhood for advice. And as you could imagine, I had to learn the hard way that just because a person is older than you doesn't necessarily mean that they are brighter.

However, I grew up very fast. I even learned how to drive a car before I could even ride a bike. I was probably the only boy in the neighborhood who couldn't ride a bicycle at the age of 12. But that didn't matter, because I was the only one of us who could drive, was having sex on the regular, and got mad respect from the older hustlers around the way. It seemed like all of the O G's in my hood wanted to take me under their wings.

I guess you could say that I didn't want to do anything that wouldn't be beneficial to my near future. Even going to school was just another excuse for me to leave the house, most of the time; and all I would do in school was flirt with the girls. You could've called me the class clown, but in a ladies man kind of way. I acted a fool in front of whoever: the teachers, the school principal, even security. I didn't care who's feelings got hurt along the way, as long as I could get at least one girl to smile my job was complete, and that was considered a good day at school.

I was never considered a pretty boy growing up; especially growing up in the 1990's when light skinned boys were in style like the newest pair of Air Jordan's. I would have to put in extra work to get my women; besides, I only aimed for the finest girls at school. Even though I wasn't a pretty boy, I was still one of the biggest players in Dickenson Middle. The preppy pretty boys would have their prissy little girlfriends, and we young gangsters would have all of their girlfriends as well as all of the good girls who loved a bad guy.

Actually, I lost my virginity to a white girl name Tracy. Back then a black guy messing with a white girl was considered lame; but, only I could pull something like this off and still be considered a player. Tracy was cool though, even though she had braces. She ran with the stuck-up black girls and was a cheerleader. Tracy was probably the coolest white girl in the school; just because she hung around black girls all of the time and still always acted like a white girl. That was what made her stand out so much; that, and the fact that she was fully developed at the age of 13. She was a year older than me and already experienced in the sex department. That girl put it on me day in and day out. After school, on our lunch breaks in the school bathrooms: everywhere! It had got to the point where she was possessive of me.

I had gotten into so much trouble my 8th grade year that the principal decided it would be in the best interest of the school if they put me on half days. They called me and like 6 other students into his office at the same time and told us the bad news. They said that we will be able to go on to high school as scheduled, but were not welcome to the middle school graduation, and that for the duration of our school year we would be required to go for half a day and to attend a special class for the insubordinate.

The funny thing is that almost all of us hung around each other every day in school anyway, so now it was like we were free to skip school every day and hang out up at the high school. Among the group of insubordinates was Money. Money was another knuckle head at the school, but we never really talked no further than saying what's up in the hallways. He had a sneaky gangster look about himself; always wearing red and braids in his hair. Money was a true gangster; you could tell by the way he carried himself. Not to mention that he would sometimes drive to middle school in a pimped out Cadillac or Trans AM. Once we started going on half days from school together, we started to hang out together every day.

We would leave school every day to go up to the E K mini mart to hang out with the high school kids on their lunch breaks. Everybody who thought they were somebody would be up at the mini mart during the LaSalle high school lunch breaks. Even though LaSalle was on the North Side of South Bend, people would come from everywhere just for the lunch breaks.

Here we were still in middle school and directly in the mix of everything. Not to mention the fact that my brother Romelo was a freshman at LaSalle; and, my sister Renea had an older sister on her mother's side that was a sophomore there too:

her name was Pooh Bear. I was well connected and knew everybody.

You see I was from the North Side of South Bend. Money was from the West Side of town. We were both a part of the Vice Lord Gang, but the North Side Vice Lords were called Conservatives; while the West Side Vice Lords were call the Insane. This really didn't make any difference, because if push came to shove we were obligated to ride or die for each other and everybody else that represented the five. Money and myself started to hang out tough together after school; both of us with our bright red colors on, wearing our hats cocked to the left with nothing to lose.

I had another really good friend that I had grown up with named Tyrone. Tyrone was one of those fat kids in the neighborhood that wasn't at all embarrassed about his weight. Actually, Tyrone was the most confident of our little north side clique. That confidence would take him a long way in life. Tyrone kept him a beautiful woman in his life, and unlike me, he took school and relationships seriously. Still, this was my best friend in the world, and one that I will always be able to count on to have my back throughout my life.

The funny thing about Tyrone is that all of my family would tell me to stop hanging around him like he was the trouble maker or something; not realizing that it was me who was always the one that brought trouble around. Please don't get me wrong though: everybody played their part in keeping the trouble going. Tyrone was just the obvious one to blame because whenever I got into trouble he was around, and I stayed in trouble.

Tyrone had two other brothers: Bryan, who was the youngest and craziest, and Shane, his older brother who went to the military at a very young age. They too grew up in a house without a father present, but their responsibility was tremendous. They were considered young men in my eyes, because at the ages of 9, 11, and 14 they were responsible to take care of their entire household. Their mother had MS and did the best she could to be a strong mother to three young boys barely mobile.

Mrs. B was her name; she was the mother of the entire North Side. Mrs. B would brighten up any day by simply showing us that no matter what cards we get dealt; that life was worth playing them with all of our heart. We all loved and respected Mrs. B. God bless her soul!

Tyrone lived around the corner from me and was only one year younger than me. We were always really good friends from the very first day we met. If a day went by that we wouldn't see each other we at least talked on the phone to find out why. People in our neighborhood always looked at me like the ruff one out of our clique, but knew that if you mess with him you mess with me. Then you had the neighborhood bullies that would mess with us all.

The North Side consisted of a few different cliques; the Humboldt Street Hustlers, which we claimed; and the Huey Street gangsters. The Humboldt Street and Huey Streets cross each other so we formed a clique call the H-Town to solidify the two. Huey Street was the older gangsters from the North Side while we were all young, dumb, and full of cum. We were the ones carrying pistols and acting a fool, so they embraced us knowing that they had young triggers at their disposal. They were getting money and maintaining respect from the blood shed we provided. That shit got old quick!

## **Chapter 3**

One day after school Money asked me if I wanted to ride with him to the West Side. He told me that his O G was supposed to get out of prison, and that he wanted me to meet him.

I accepted his offer, but was a little nervous because I had never known anybody who got out of prison before. All of my guys who went to prison went for murder and Robbery, so by the time they get out I will be an old man. This will be the first time I've ever been around a person who came home.

His O G's name was Red, and to my surprise he was nothing like what I expected. He was very laid back and treated me like I was family. Red was 24 years old, and had just got done serving a 6 year bit. Even though he was almost twice our age he treated us like we were grown, and treated Money like his own son.

Red was a player in all senses of the word. After doing over two years of lifting weights he was cock diesel. From the time we arrived at his mother's house, girl after girl came by to see him and to bring his children to see their father: Red had 8 children, with two on the way by girls he got pregnant while in prison.

Red was a true pretty boy, but not like one I had ever met before, because he was a thug. He had really curly hair and greenish brown eyes; he was about 6 feet tall and about 225 pounds. He was definitely cool to hang around. Very calm and in control at all times, even when three of his girlfriends was at his party at the same time. I respected the player in him.

I immediately took a liking to Red and knew that I would learn a lot from him from the first day we met. From the beginning to the end of his and Moneys conversation, he was talking about getting paid and how he was going to really put it down tough this time. To me it all sounded like foreign language, but still, even in Chinese I could tell that I wanted to get a part of what ever they were talking about. I stayed in my place though, and waited my turn: which I knew would come eventually.

A couple of Red's homeboys threw him a barbecue up at Kennedy Park; so, me and Money just sat back and had a blast. Other than Red constantly teasing me about being from the North Side, the whole day was a cool experience.

After Money and I left the party, I was buzzed off of beer.

"What did Red mean by putting it down tough?" I asked Money.

"Hustling," Money replied keeping it short and simple. He looked at me in a way like I might be the police before looking back at the road again.

"Hustling?" I asked him again with a dumbfound look on my face.

I knew right then and there that my homeboy Money was on a whole other level. Here I was still stealing bikes and cloths from Targets and my classmate is talking about 'hustling' with grown folks; the language of the streets. Immediately, I started asking Money question after question, and to my surprise he knew all of the answers. Money was game tight; he told me about how he used to make moves and pretty much run things for Red as a young buck. I was in astonishment by how much this young nigga knew about the streets.

On the walk home from the West Side that night, which was about a mile, I was ecstatic. I couldn't wait to tell all of my homeys about this new way of hustling I was just introduced to; but, to my surprise nobody cared about selling drugs. To all of my homeys, selling drugs was unheard of; everybody knew a crack head when we seen one, but to actually approach one about selling them stuff was just plain disrespectful. I just kind of left it alone, because they were all right; here I was barely 13 years old and ready to get involved in a game that there was no turning back from.

I still continued to hang out with Money; we hung out with Red just about everyday. Red was temporarily working at a construction job so that he could save up a few checks to cop with, so most of the days after school, Money and I would hang out up at E K or over Money's grandmothers house. I loved hanging out at Money's house, because usually his grandmother or older brother would send us to the store in one of their cars. Money's grandmother's car was a forest green 1979 Fleetwood Brougham; and his brother had a cherry red Pontiac Trans AM.

At the age of 14 Money drove like a straight up pimp; he would swing around corners making Cadillac turns all over the place. I was always amazed at the way Money drove; he was shorter than me, so when he was behind the wheel, it would look like the car was driving all by its self. Money is the one who taught me how to "Cadillac Pimp" cars like him. I always thought I could drive; but, Money showed me how to let the car flow and how to become a part of the road with the car. Money taught me everything he knew about the streets: from diving to dressing like a player. Money changed my life around, so if I was to give credit to anybody for my lifestyle, it would have to be Money.

Money's older brother's name was Mike Mike. Mike Mike was the craziest person that I had ever met. Mike was a Gangster Disciple; better know as a G D on the streets. G Ds are the Vice Lords greatest rivals, so when I first heard that Money's older brother was a G D, I was confused. Money didn't fool with his brother or look up to him at all; to Money, Red was his role model. I guess the fact that him and his brother was 10 years apart made a big difference, but still, I never quite understood why they weren't close at all.

Maybe I am wrong, but I was always under the impression that Mike Mike and Red were in competition to gain Money's respect. Mike Mike and Red didn't fool with each other either, even though they grew up together; but, they still had a lot of respect for each other. I think that deep down inside, I always liked Mike Mike more than Red; especially after I got to know Mike Mike better.

Mike was a more suave type of player than anything I had ever seen before. He would wine and dine women; send flowers and candies to there jobs; and, I even seen him put his Wilson's leather jacket on the ground so his girlfriend wouldn't step in a puddle of water once.

*The Son of the Streets...*
*Terrence leRoy Baker*

I think that the fact that Mike Mike wasn't a pretty boy like Red, and that he was more of a ruff neck type of mack, made me relate to his style more. He would always keep the finest of women; not taking anything from Red, because he had fine women too; but, Red didn't have to run game or romance his women the way Mike Mike did. Just being a pretty boy back in the 1990's was enough.

Still the fact stands that when you run game and really put in work to get your women's attention; they are the women who end up really caring about you and last forever: if you so choose. Mike Mike taught me his way of running game and how romancing women is the only way to get long term results out of them, and also that romancing is the foundation that pimping was built on.

As you can see, I had a lot of respect for them both, and still do. I learned a lot from them, by simply being observant and asking questions. Mike Mike and Red were like night and day: Mike Mike was loud and wild; Red was quiet, laid back, and sneaky. From hanging out with money, I got the best of both worlds; not to mention the fact that Money taught me a lot too about the streets.

## Chapter 4

That school year went by fast. Before we new it Money and I were enjoying the summer. For me and the rest of the eighth graders, that meant that our next school year will be held at none other than the infamous LaSalle High School. After the last day of school I went to Money's house. Neither one of us was invited to the school graduation, so we had our own celebration at his house.

Later on that after noon I had gotten a phone call from my mother. My mother told me that my brother had gotten into a horrible car accident while riding on his friend's mo-pad after school.

I'll never forget that day, because Money was the one who took me up to the hospital to see him. Up until I had met Money, everything that I did I did following in my brothers foot steps. We had the same friends; wore the same clothes; and, we even shared girlfriends from time to time. I looked to him for everything.

My brother was the opposite of me, he was smooth and seemed to do everything right. I was the clumsy one that nobody acknowledged: especially on my father's side. My mother was really the only person who treated us equally. Everybody else would treat me like I was a tag along.

I even remember one day when one of my aunties on my father's side said, "You're not even really your father's son, your mother got pregnant with you while she was gone off to college, so you can't be his son." Those words pierced my soul for life, and it was from that moment on that my mother stopped letting us visit our grandparents house on the weekends. Could you imagine being 7 years old and being told that everything you stood for was a lie? I will never forgive her for telling me that; even though it wasn't true, because it took 20 years for me to find out the truth.

Sitting there at the hospital looking at my older brother, who was always my personal hero, in such a bad position made tears come to my eyes. I would've traded my life to get him out of that situation that he was in. My brother was partially paralyzed from the waste down. The doctors said that he would probably never be able to walk again. The way my brother looked at me so helplessly and said, "You're the man of the house now" just broke my heart.

That summer was different from any other summer of my life. Not only was my brother in the hospital, but I was on a whole different mission. I was spending most of my time away from the hood, because with out my older brother around, I felt out of place.

Tyrone and his brothers started to hang out with J C and his older brother Joe who moved back to South Bend from New Jersey that summer; they form a rap group called Mad Evil. I couldn't rap, nor had any interest in rapping at all, so I was just an out caster. They all made up little rap names for themselves, but I didn't have one so I just stayed away. Joe was a few years older than all of us so he got all of them to start smoking weed and drinking too. I didn't do any smoking or drinking with them because I didn't want to seem like I was following anybody.

When my brother did finally get released from the hospital, he was on a walker. He was a pretty good rapper too, so every day we would walk all the way around to Tyrone's house so he could go into Tyrone's basement to rap. They call the basement the Madd Evil Asylum, and had it popping off. My brother would get all high and drunk, then I would have to carry him home on my back because he would be too high to walk on his walker. I was like the designated walker for him, which I never really minded; I just hated to see my brother let go of himself the way he did.

One day I went over Tyrone's house without my brother there and one of J C and Joes cousins was over there. He had got high and started to talk about me, telling me I was the weakest link. I had had enough, so I put the hands on him, not knowing that everybody in the basement was going to jump in to beat me up: even my best friend Tyrone.

Here I was the dude that Tyrone and his brothers all grew up with, and they jumped me. Shane was the only one who didn't jump in, I appreciated it. However, I didn't get hut badly because it was about 10 of them all trying to jump on me at once.

When I got home and told my brother about it, he was hurt. It hurt him more that he couldn't do anything about it than the fact that it happened.

I called Money the next day and the first thing he said was to come get his pistol and go bust a cap in all of their asses. I was definitely not ready for all of that, so I politely declined his offer. Then I told him that I was going to walk over there.

"What? You ain't got to walk my nigga. I can get my brothers car and come get you. Wait until you see what he did to it." Money told me,

"Shit, he been asking me where you disappeared to anyway."

"Are you Serious?" I said feeling important.

I will be there in about 15 minutes," Money said before hanging up.

"Terry!" my mother yelled to me into my bedroom.

"Yes!"

"That boy is out side for you," she told me knowing that I was expecting Money.

My mother failed to mention the fact that he was inside his brothers cherry red Trans AM with the T-tops off; and, with some triple gold Daytona rims on it. The car was amazing to me! I couldn't believe that his brother even let him drive it to come get me. I felt like a big shot just to be getting picked up inside it.

My mother told me who it was once I came out from the back, and then she gave me that look to tell me to be careful. My mother always did like Money; I think it was because of the fact that he never tried to act all goodie two shoes in front of her like all of my other friends did. He knew he was bad, but just no worst than anybody else, so you had to respect him for his honesty: I guess anyway.

When I came out of the house all of the girls from on my block was waving at me and showing special interest in me like I was somebody to be cool with just because I was riding in an exotic car like that. I knew then that one day I had to have me an exotic car of my own: possibly a Trans AM with T- tops on it too.

"Man, what in the world was your brother thinking letting you drive this machine to come get me?" I asked Money getting into the passenger seat.

"Please, he was letting me drive, so why would he stop now just because he hooked it up? Wait until you hear the system he put in here" Money told me speeding off from in front of my house.

We rode around the hood for a while; passing by Tyrone's house several times. All of the same people that had jumped me the prior day were in front of his house waving at me like we were best of friends in the world. I even waved back, what the hell. I was on top of the world and wanted to enjoy my fifteen minutes of fame. What better revenge then to be seen in an exotic machine like the one I was in with my homeboy from the West Side.

Finally we made it back to Money's house where it seemed like his brother
Mike Mike was waiting in the middle of the street for us to return safely.

"What's up Terry? Do you like what I did to the ride?" Mike asked me.

"Do I like it? I love it?" I said to him speechlessly. I still could barely speak from the loud music blasting in my ear and the fact that Money was averaging 100 miles an hour.

Money's pager was beeping like crazy, so he went in the house to use the phone; I stayed outside to talk to Mike Mike while he washed up his car for the night. I offered to help him out, but he quickly declined my offer saying that I might scratch it up, and then he would have to kill me. I believed that he would too.

Mike Mike was far from slow, so once he realized that I wasn't trying to wash his car for free, he smiled at me, and then told me I was a little hustler in the making. Then he offered to take me out riding with him later on when he rolled out to the club. I quickly accepted.

I ran into the house to tell Money about the good news, but when I ran up into his bedroom I saw him doing something important and waited to tell him. He was using a scale to weight up something; and, for some reason I had a good idea what that something was.

Money saw me looking at him and immediately started to explain the whole process to me. At that time he was weighing up a twenty rock, which was just a small piece of rock the size of a bread crumb. From the looks of the piece that he was breaking them off of, I could tell that he could make a lot of twenties out of it.

I had forgotten all about going out with Mike Mike; instead, I was interested in learning how to break up and baggage crack cocaine. Money was good at teaching me too; he told me how he met the people that he was selling it to through Red, and how it all worked. After he explained it all to me, I came to the assumption that Red gave him all of his business, so it basically all sounded pretty easy. However, I did have one huge problem. How could I make any money if Red was all the way on the West Side and I lived on the North? Plus, he never included me into his little hustle to begin with, so how was I supposed to get involve with out overstepping my boundaries. I couldn't just walk up to him and ask, because I would be out of line, because he didn't know or trust me the way he did Money.

I just sat back in amazement at how much I learned about selling drugs in just a few minutes.

"What did you want to tell me when you came running upstairs about to lose your mind," Money asked me not taking his eyes off of the drugs.

"Oh, Mike is going to take me out with him tonight." I said nonchalantly.

Money looked at me in a concerned kind of way and said, "Where did he say he was taking you to?"

I felt the concern that Money had immediately and almost changed my mind about going all together, "What I shouldn't go?"

He just finished up what he was doing and told me, "That's up to you. Just be careful, and don't let him get you all high." I felt like a child going on my first date; but I still took everything he told me seriously.

"I need to make a couple of runs. Do you want to come with me?" Money asked me to take my mind off of the stuff he had just told me to spoil my surprise.

"Sure," I said snapping out of the trance I was in.

We left on foot going God knows where in his neighborhood. I sat back and observed Money make move after move. Sometimes we went to peoples houses; others we just met cars as they rode by us walking down the street. Each and every time though, Money was in complete control of the situation. I even heard him cussing one or two of them out for being short with their money; but, no matter how short they came, or if they didn't give him any money at all, they still walked away happy.

Daylight turned into night, and before I knew it, it was past 8:00 pm when we got back to his house. Mike Mike wasn't there, for a minute I was a little disappointed. Then I helped Money count up all of $500 dollars. We had to count up the money ten times before Money was satisfied. Then we walked down to Reds house were Money gave him almost all of the money except $25 dollars; then he ordered us some pizza with that.

A few minutes after the pizza made it to Money's house; I heard Mike Mike flying down the street blasting the new Scarface album. All I could hear was the bass bumping through the whole house. As soon as Mike Mike came into the house my adrenaline started pumping in my veins. He had left his car running outside, so you could only hear the dual exhaust pipes and a low bass pumping from the turned down stereo system.

Mike Mike went into the basement were his room was to get dressed for the evening, and then came flying back upstairs and out of the door without saying one word to me. It was as if he never made any plans to take me anywhere with him. For a minute I felt stood up like a women on her first date.

"He does be full of it some of the times, but if he said he was taking you out with him he probably will," Money said with a mouth full of pizza and knowing how I must have been felling.

"How do you know?" I asked in a frustrated way.

"Shit, because he is my brother!" Money yelled at me causing us both to break out into laughter.

"Hey, Terry," Mike Mike yelled for me from outside knowing that I was probably looking out of the window at him. "Come on before you get left!"

"See, I told you so," Money said happy for me. "But, don't forget what I told you about getting high and shit."

"I won't," I reassured him. "Thanks for the pizza."

"What? You better take a couple slices with you, because I can't eat all of it by myself," he told me.

## The Son of the Streets...
### Terrence leRoy Baker

    I jumped up and went for the door not knowing or caring what I was getting myself into. Nervously, I got into the car and waited for Mike Mike to finish talking to his friend in the middle of the street. All I could think about was how I was in a way betraying Money; but, still, it was my time to get a chance to shine, and Mike Mike asked me to come, so I had no choice in the matter.

## **<u>Chapter 5</u>**

As soon as Mike Mike jumped into the car he threw the car into gear and sped off in one fluent motion like a bat out of hell. The music was blasting and I was scared as hell. Mike Mike drove like a mad man. Money drove wild, but Mike Mike drove plain crazy. You could tell that they learned how to drive from the same place, which I later found out, was the true speed demon: Their mother.

It took me a while to adjust to the whole scene, and that wasn't easy considering the fact that the windows were so darkly tinted. My seat was leaned so far back that I couldn't look at anything else other than the stars in the sky that were easily visible through the open T-tops. Mike Mike was waving at every car that rolled by us, he was like a ghetto celebrity. Every five minutes he would roll down both windows and yell out of the car at the women and men alike who were eager for his attention.

Now what really was tripping me out the most was the fact that Mike Mike had on a leather jacket and it was in mid summer; he also had on some dark loc sunglasses that with the dark tint on the windows had to make it impossible to see anything. I thought he was a lunatic.

For the first hour or so we didn't say a word to each other, which would've been practically impossible over the loud music. All we did was fly across city streets stopping at every gas station and liquor store along the way.

After about the tenth stop, Mike Mike came out of a house that he was inside for over 45 minutes. The music was all the way down, and I had almost fallen asleep waiting for him.

"You smoke weed?" Mike Mike asked me out of the blue.

"No!" I said in a laid back young way. He just smirked at me like a devil in disguise.

"Well I hope you don't mind," he said while lighting up his pre rolled joint. "If you do that's just too bad!"

"Why doesn't Money put you down? You seem like a cool little nigga?" Mike asked me catching me completely off guard.

"I don't know, but maybe he will one day if Red let him," I said a little embarrassed.

"Do you know what you are doing?" He asked me while choking on his weed.

"Yeah, sure," I lied to him trying to look cooler than I really was, and having no clue what I was about to get myself into.

"Well I will tell you what, you are going to be my little nigga. I am going to put you down with me," he said feeling like a king.

I didn't say anything to that at all. The best way to call a persons bluff is through silence. He brought me the proposition, so I was going to see if he would keep his word about it. It all seemed too good to be true. Mike Mike just smiled at me knowing that I wasn't a bit scared of a challenge.

After about another hour he dropped me off at Money's house and gave me my first package. I followed him down into his dungeon and was amazed at how it was all pimped out down there. My first package was an eight ball, or should I say it was supposed to be. Mike Mike didn't even use a scale to weigh it. He just broke off a chunk of rock and told me I owed him $125.

I looked at it quickly, and before I showed him that I had never touched any dope before, I shoved it into my pocket. Still standing there half expecting him to give me a beeper or somebody to sell it to, he cut off the light and left to finish his late night creep. We shook hands in a nice to do business kind of way, all I was thinking about was how I was about to get myself killed.

After Mike Mike left I went upstairs to Money's room, where he already had a pillow and blanket laid out for me on the floor. I went to sleep immediately, ready to get up so that I could figure out how not to get myself killed.

The next morning I woke up from a dream that my beeper was going off, but it was Money's. I jumped up to tell Money about my night. After I used the bathroom and brushed my teeth, I came back into the room catching Money with his scale out, so I started to tell him what happened. Before I could tell him about my night he told me the whole story like he had been through it a million times before.

Once he got done telling me the story of my night I told him about the dope Mike Mike had given me. I pulled out my rock that he gave me and put it on Money's scale, and to both of our surprise it was 4.5 grams. It was way more than a normal eight ball.

"How much did he charge you for this?" Money asked not at all impressed. Maybe he was even a little bit jealous.

"$125," I told him.

"Not bad, but where are you going to sell it at, because I can't help you sell it. I work for Red, and he would be pissed off." Money told me reading my mind.

"Well, can I use your scale to break it down into twenties?" I asked disappointedly.

"Sure, but if I was you I would make a couple of dimes and fifties too," he added to let me know that he was still my homeboy. This was just business.

Deep down inside I knew he didn't think that I could sell it anyway, and to tell the truth, neither did I. But, I was sure going to try.

## <u>Chapter 6</u>

On the walk home I was scared to death. I kept putting my hand inside of my pocket to see if my dope packs were still there. It was as if I thought that they would just jump out and walk away from me. I had seen several potential customers, but was afraid to approach them. That was the longest walk home I ever took.

At first I didn't tell anybody, not even my brother. I was afraid of the truth: the fact that I had no idea what I was doing or where to start. Later on that night Tyrone came by my house. He acted like he was simply walking down my street, but I knew better. Even though I was still a little mad at him about our little incident at his house, I forgave him instantly.

After we talked about what happened for a while, he told me about how everybody in the hood saw me with Money. I figured that was a good opportunity to tell him about my dilemma.

"Guess what? I got hooked up on that thing I was telling you about before," I told him out of the blue.

"What little thing are you talking about? You always talking," Tyrone said laughing.

"You know what thing I am talking about. The drug things fool!" I said impatiently.

"Oh! What about it?" He asked.

"I got hooked up on that," I told him.

I showed him what I had inside of my pocket. Then I also told him about everything else that happened and all that I learned from Money on how to weigh it up and all. After I explained everything to him I told him the bad news: that I didn't have anybody to sell it to and how I was scared I will get killed if I did sell it.

"Man with all of these crack heads on your block, you mean to tell me that you don't have anybody to sell it to," Tyrone said laughing in my face. "Shit, I will help you go to every one of their houses on the block, and sell it with you if you buy me and you a pizza like Money did. I am hungry than a hostage."

"If we can sell it all before I die, I will also give you twenty dollars to go with that pizza, because if I am adding my money up right, I can make about $450 off of it," I said in a cocky way.

"Damn nigga, I know we aren't on best terms, but you're only going to give me $20 out of how much?" Tyrone said laughing. "Well, I guess it is about twenty dollars more than what I got right now so fuck it lets get money."

We started off at this white guy name Dale's house. Dale was a known crack head in the neighborhood. He would fix on all of the drug dealers cars and even fix our bike tires for us growing up. He thought we were crazy when we first told him what we had.

Dale didn't have any money, but we still gave him a dime rock to try it out for us. Then we went back down in front of my house and waited for something to happen. We hung out for about an hour before we saw Dale again, but this time he was with another one of my neighbors named Kim. The whole night went like this. Dale went to everybody on my block for us, and everybody that he brought to us brought somebody else back with them. Before the night was up, we had sold all of the dope that I had and were about $400 richer, with $50 out on credit until payday.

      I kept my word and gave Tyrone his $20, but it was too late to order a pizza. We just called it a night, and I made a promise that I would buy us breakfast in the morning. Tyrone didn't care about any pizza; he was 13 years old with money to blow in his pocket. He was ready for the world, and couldn't wait for me to put him down so we could do the same thing we did on his block that we just did on mine. The whole North Side was full of streets like ours, so there were a lot of doors to knock on and a lot of money to be made.

## Chapter 7

That next morning I woke up ecstatic. I didn't know how I did it, but I sold all of the dope in one day. I felt like a true kingpin! The feeling of success that I got from my first date with drugs changed my whole outlook on life.

I beeped Money early that morning; he called back immediately expecting some bad news, but there was none. He told me that he had talked to Red about me; but, the way he said it was like they laughed at me or didn't believe that I would succeed in the drug game. Then he made it clear that Red didn't want him helping me sell the drugs.

"Is Mike Mike there?" I asked nonchalantly.

"Yeah, but he sleep. Why?" Money asked. "What's wrong?"

"Nothing!" I said in a get out of my business sort of way.

"Man you know Mike still sleep. Do you want me to wake him up or something?" Money asked.

"No, it's cool. I am about to walk over there," I said in a way to see if my good friend would come pick me up.

"Alright, if he wakes up I will tell him you are on your way through," he said showing me that he wasn't feeling me at all.

I knew right then that Money wanted to be involved in our conversation; half way hoping that I messed up, but more so proud of me if I didn't. He was even more interested by me not telling him what was going on. I guess I learned at an early age to control a situation into my advantage.

Before I was able to get out of the house good Tyrone was walking up the street. He couldn't wait until today either. He had plans of his own, and he saw a bright future full of ways to see his plans follow through.

"What's up?" I said.

"Shit, a nigga came to get his breakfast that is owed to him," he said making us both break out into laughter.

"Oh, I almost forgot all about that. You might as well walk to the West Side with me then, because I am on my way over there right now," I said offering him along with me for the first time. "Besides, you can use the exercise."

"Fuck you!" Tyrone said laughing at my not so funny fat joke.

At first I thought about not bringing him along, but felt like he was as much of a part of my success as a drug dealer as I was. If he wouldn't have ever come over and hyped me up to approach Dale, I would still have the same sack of rocks with me on the long journey across town. He was my partner, and right hand man.

On the way we stopped at Popeye's Chicken. Popeye's was down the street from my house and on the way to the West Side. Everybody at Popeye's knew us because we grew up eating free chicken there.

As soon as we entered, the ladies started getting us a small sack ready. But, when we place our orders they just smiled and treated us like normal paying customers. Everybody in the neighborhood loved Tyrone and me, so even though we were paying, they still made sure to give us plenty extra to show us that we would still be treated like the children of the streets that we are.

Tyrone is a big boy, so I ordered us a family size meal. I spent over $10 dollars on it, which was more than I had ever spent at a restaurant before on one meal, but was well worth it and we enjoyed every cent.

We ate and laughed for over an hour. We talked about girls, school, and everything else under the sun. After we had stuffed ourselves to the point of intoxication, we decided to leave. An older guy from our neighborhood saw us enjoying ourselves and decided to give us a lift, which we surely needed because there was no way we was going to walk across town as stuffed as we were.

We got dropped off in front of Money's house, but he was down the street at Red's. He yelled for me to come down there, and just like always, everybody greeted each other. I introduced Tyrone, and then everybody went back to talking around him the same way they did me the first time.

Even though I had already put Tyrone up on game, he didn't say a word. While they thought he was lost, he was absorbing the game: the whole swagger, which he could see I already had down to a tee.

Tyrone wasn't at all impressed with them, but was amazed by me and the way I was carrying myself. The fact that they kept trying to hint at my dope selling experience and I never said anything to them about what happened the previous night. I had a pocket full of money, and like it did most people, the money didn't change me one bit. I am sure he noticed how they both talked to me in a way like I was a fool, but the best way to catch a sucker is to play the sucker, so I played on enjoying the show.

While they all laughed at jokes that weren't that funny; I stayed myself. When they wanted me to feel like I was one of them; I stayed myself. I never once acted better than Tyrone, or anyone else I ever hung out with. I just played along, gaining a trust and loyalty from Tyrone that could never be broken apart. Tyrone just sat there and watched how the game changes so many people, and understood how it was possible.

After a while Mike Mike drove down the street in the green Cadillac. He flew right past us all without waving. I went down to their house and let myself in.

"Money," Money's grandmother called out. "That boy is here!"

"Sorry Grandma, but I am looking for Mike Mike," I said to her.

"It doesn't matter. They both the same to me," she said causing us both to start laughing.

Sure enough Mike Mike answered her, and came running upstairs. He stopped in his tracks as soon as he saw it was me waiting on him.

"We need to talk," I told him adding icing to his already nervous cake.

"What's wrong?" he asked in an 'I am not going to kill you if you messed up kind of way.'

"Nothing is wrong. I am done and got your money," I said.

"Oh yeah! Money had me all nervous talking about you had some bad news for me," he told me relieved.

So I paid him his money and was ready for my next package. Unfortunately for me he didn't have another pack to give me. My heart dropped when he told me that he was all out and would be for the next few days. I had people waiting on me, plus I told Tyrone that I would put him on this time too. Even though I was mad I played it off cool and went back down to Red's house where I had left Tyrone all alone with him and Money.

Everybody was waiting on me to say something, because from the look on my face, I had just got dealt a bad hand of poker.

"What happened?" Money finally asked still thinking that I must have messed up the money or something bad.

"Nothing, I paid Mike Mike his money, but now he is all out of dope, and I have tons of people waiting on me," I said throwing the last part in to catch Red's attention.

"Man that's some bullshit, I got people waiting on me too," Tyrone said out of the blue.

They all looked at quiet Tyrone like he had just cursed in the middle of a church sermon. Hearing him say that he also had people waiting on him proved that they had totally underestimated him, and most of all hearing me say that I had sold all of the work overnight made them both look at me in a strange way.

"You sold all of that shit in one day?" Money asked me in a proud way.

"Well, it wasn't a lot really. We sold it all in a couple of hours. The North Side is rolling," I said nonchalantly.

Red just smiled at us all knowing that he could make everything all right. He also knew that I was desperate. He saw a natural; a young nigga who had just got that first piece of action and made that first dollar. He knew how I felt, because he too felt that same feeling. It puts a certain kind of hunger in a person's eyes: a sense of having power over your own destiny.

"It felt better than sex didn't it?" Red asked me out of nowhere still feeling my pain.

"Yes, it did!" I replied knowing exactly what him asking me that question must have meant.

That was it. There was nothing else to be said. It was a done deal right then and there after those spoken words of passion towards the game. They say that a true boss' word is law and that his suggestions are orders. Well right then and there I knew I was in the presence of a boss, and that he looked at me in my eyes knowing that one day I will be one too, but not realizing that that day was already here.

Red had hooked me up as expected. Even though he was nice about it, he still charged me $150 for less than what Mike Mike gave me for $125. Then I asked him to take me up to Sherman's to purchase a beeper on the way to drop us off on the North Side.

"Yeah, I will take you. Do you have some money?" Red asked me in a way that told me that if I didn't he wasn't going to pay for it.

"Yeah, I got some money!" I said offended. "How much do they cost anyway?"

Red just looked over into the passenger seat at Money who shrugged his shoulders when asked where he found me at. I could tell that Money was really starting to look at me differently. He liked my style. You could also tell that Money was the one who told Red about me, and that it was him who was making all of this possible for me. Money was rooting for me the whole time. I felt a sense of respect for my young O G who had taught me the basics of the game.

Tyrone just sat in the back seat looking at me with a smile on his face. He was enjoying himself and learning at the same time. Seeing me barring none, staying myself, and even treating him with love and respect after he betrayed me in his basement, was proof that I was mentally on another level for my age. Maybe you could say that with the dope game you have no choice but to grow up overnight and that seems like what happened to us both.

We were in Reds 69 Impala. The car was immaculate. It was cocaine white with a baby blue soft top with the matching interior; hammers and vogues for its shoes and socks; and dual exhausts playing a song of its own that sounded like Barry White's classic 'I am going to give you all of my love.' That on top of the extremely loud speakers in the trunk made the car sound like gorillas where trying to jump out of there. We both sat back in awe!

We all went inside Sherman's where everybody in South Bend purchased their beepers and cell phones acting like we owned the place. I felt larger than life knowing that I could afford to purchase one no matter how much they cost. To my surprise they didn't cost much at all. So, I purchased me one, and helped Tyrone who didn't hesitate one minute to use his only $20 to make an investment in his own career. I forked over the other $20 and he insisted that as soon as he made some money that he would reimburse me. I knew then that Tyrone was a natural for this game. Even though I could've afforded to buy us both beepers that were nicer than the one Money had, I decided not to. One of the 48 Laws of Power insists not to ever out shine the master, so we kept it simple and chose the one that he had.

Red just watched all three of us in remembrance of when he was our age. For a second you would've thought that he felt bad, but then the second was gone when he decided to treat us all to Ponderosa on the way home. After all, we wanted it for ourselves; he never pushed it down our throats. He just made sure that we knew what we where doing so that we didn't get ourselves messed over the way the game is known for messing over the weak.

At Ponderosa which is an all you can eat steak house and buffet, Red ordered us all T- bone steaks. Even though Tyrone and I were still stuffed from earlier, we still grubbed on the delicious steak dinners.

By the time we got back to the hood it was dark outside. Still, everyone on the block was in the streets playing. We both got out of the car like ghetto superstars: beepers on our hips, full and ready for a long night on the streets.

When I walked into my house, my mother was cooking. She told me that Dale came over to tell me that my bike was fixed, which she knew was a lie because I didn't even own a bike. Then I told her that I had a beeper and gave her the number.

She just looked at me knowing that her baby boy was becoming a man and choosing which path to take in his life. Of course she was disappointed in my choice of lifestyle, but at the same time she knew that she would never have to hold my hand again. My mother was and always will be my best friend in the world. I knew that I could tell her anything and that she wouldn't ever judge me, but only help me anyway that she could. Little did I know the lifestyle that I chose would have the opposite effect on my life, because not only will she have to hold my hand again, but more often then not.

I stood there taller than she had ever seen me stand before, but at that one instant, she let go of me; washed her hands of my stubbornness, my lack of understanding of the world, and all of the mess ups in school. She let me live the life that I so chose for myself knowing that one day I would be back, hoping that it wouldn't be too late. I was on my own from that moment on and I didn't even know it yet; unaware that one choice can and will map out a persons' future.

A tear came running down my face; breaking the silent conversation that I just had with the only person I knew how to love unconditionally.

"Straighten yourself up boy," my mother told me.

I smiled feeling like I had just told my darkest secret to my girlfriend, and knowing that she understood, and that the honesty brought us even closer together.

Tyrone was standing right there the whole time, witnessing my life change in front his face. He saw my mother and I hold such a deep conversation with out using any words. He too had eyes full of tears and a heart full of respect because he knew that I couldn't turn back now and that he still could, but didn't want to. He wanted that hustle, that respect, and that since of power that came only from the streets at such a young age. We both wanted the same thing!

## **Chapter 8**

My mother was dating a white man by the name of Jim whom she worked at Notre Dame with. He was a nice man. One Christmas he bought us all a pair of shoes with a matching outfit, but other than that we didn't see much of him.

Jim also had three other children of his own that he had full custody of. He was the first man I believe I'd ever seen take care of two boys and a little girl on his own. All of his children were mixed from a previous marriage.

Jim's children were all younger than us and they were mixed. So even though they were raised by their father, which is even harder than being raised by a single mother, we all had a lot in common. I always wondered if it was even harder for them being raised by their white father, and not having a connection with the black side of there lives. They never felt that compassion of a mother's love, or the warmth of knowing that your mother is there whenever you needed a hug.

Instead they were raised by there father's hard love. A man can't connect to a feminine side of themselves when raising boys, and as hard as it is not to, a man can't hug and kiss you every time you fall down.

Just seeing what they were going through opened my eyes to the cold world we all lived in. It made me come to the realization that all my life when I thought we had it rough, there were people out there who had it even worse. I realized that even though we never had the whole world growing up, we had something much more precious: we had motherly love.

Here these kids are in a house where they were fortunate. Their father made great money and could fill up a Christmas tree; buy them any and everything they ever wanted on their birthdays. Still, none of those things could ever compare to the amount of love we received from our mother alone, and I wouldn't have traded it for the world.

My mother taught us how to love each other, and that we could tell her anything. She taught us that what goes on inside of our house stayed inside of our house, and that we could always trust her if not anybody else.

Meeting Jim and his children made me appreciate every Christmas and birthday present that I had ever received. That was when I came to the point in my life where I didn't care anymore about if my father loved me, or if he will ever be apart of my life. I had so much more than he could ever give me: I had a strong mother.

My mother would stay over Jim's house most of the nights out of the week. They worked together, so it was convenient, but still we did miss her at times; especially my little sister.

I was hustling good enough to order pizza or even to send somebody to McDonald's to get us all food. Sometimes, my mother would come home after work and cook simple meals, most of the time hamburger helper, but even then she would still go back over Jim's house.

We never complained, because we were still taking care of ourselves, and for the first time in our lives, it seemed like our mother was happy, so it was hard for us to complain. When the school year came back around it was even harder, because I had the freedom to sell drugs all night long and skip school all together.

I bought all of my own clothes and shoes, and would buy my lil sister both shoes and clothes too. My brother was still handicap, but he started to sell dope with me too. He would help me out at night time when I was moving around, but for the most part he didn't really care about hustling the way I did. Other than going to physical therapy, he stuck to himself most of the time. He was depressed and stressed out from not being able to walk, and I was the only person he would fool around with. Still, I would keep my distance, because I felt bad in a way; I felt like I was leaving him behind or alone. My brother was proud of me though. All my life I followed behind his shadow, so for him to see me making my own way made him proud.

Still, no matter how much money I made or whatever I accumulated in the streets, he was still my big brother and I always gave him the utmost respect.

My mother came home one day during that school year, and she told us we were moving. She told us that she had gotten married.

All of us looked at each other, and our little hearts dropped. I didn't know whether to be happy or sad, but I knew I felt left out. After I came to my senses, I congratulated her. We all did, because she was happy, so from the way we were raised it made us happy too. How could we not be happy?

Our mother and Jim had what you would call a beautiful story. A story worth reading just to see if it will have a happy ending, but hoping and praying it never ends at all, because it all seemed so perfect and meant to be. It was too good to be true!

## <u>Chapter 9</u>

That school year went by fast. We all moved together into a big house on the outskirts of the North Side. It was a big move; especially for me, because I was no longer free to move around or stay out at all hours of the night.

I was fifteen years old, and feeling grown, so there was definitely going to be problems around the house. I had an old Bonneville, but couldn't drive it home at night time. There were so many new rules to follow that I ended up put out of the house within six months time.

Sometimes I think that the rules were intentionally set so that Jim could get me put out. He knew that I was selling drugs, and he didn't want his children looking up to me. I was young and buying my own video games, clothes, and shoes. It was no secret that I had a car already either, so he had to find a way to get rid of me.

One day when I came home late, or should I say after the curfew that we were given' my mother was at the door waiting as I put my key inside. She opened it for me scaring me half to death.

"I am sorry," she told me with tears rolling down her face.

"What is wrong?" I asked in a concerned sort of way.

"I can't let you mess up my life while you throw yours away. You have to give me your key, and never return here again," she told me in such a bold way that it made my heart cold forever.

"Ma, it is cold out here, and two feet of snow on the ground. Where am I supposed to go to?" I asked not fully aware of how serious she was.

"I don't know and I don't care, just take care and try not to get killed."

That was it. She let me gather enough of my things, or at least as much as I could carry at midnight; which only included my 9 mm pistol and the little money and dope that I had which wasn't much when your fifteen years old and now homeless.

"Where are you going?" my brother asked me seeing that I was packing up my belongings.

"Ma, just put me out," I told him.

He was back to walking again and almost back to his full health. In his eyes I could tell he knew that I would make it on my own, but still he wouldn't let that happen.

"Wait a minute!" he insisted. "I am coming with you."

"You going where?" my mother asked him knowing that his health wasn't 100%.

"If he has to leave, then I am going with him," he told her.

"I figured you would say that, but you don't have to leave. I am not putting you out."

"Yes I do," was all he said.

My mother sighed. I always wondered what she would have told him if I wasn't standing there, or if she wanted him to come with me. Deep down inside I knew that my getting put out wasn't even my mothers decision; however, I never placed blame on anybody in particular. I just dealt with the cards I was being dealt.

I loved my brother to death for what he did, but still didn't want him to put himself in my situation with me. I felt horrible, yet at the same time safe.

We made it for the first week or so, but hotel rooms and eating out everyday got to be expensive. Eventually, I messed up Red's money so bad that he cut me off, and we were sleeping in cars or crack heads houses. The funny thing is at first we were welcome. But as soon as I lost my connection, even the crack heads turned us away. It was a cold winter, and we were feeling every bit of it.

Since my brother was always a playboy, he had found some girls that had a crib who let us stay with them from time to time, but I was not as welcome as he was.

I had a girlfriend named Jasmine who lived on the Lake side of town, and her mother worked the third shift. So, after 11:00 pm, I could come over her house, but still had to leave before 6:00 am.

Jasmine and I got real tight. I was with her before I got put out so we were already in a relationship with each other. Her family liked me too. All of them were originally from California, so I thought they were cool. The first time I ever went over to Jasmine's house I found a trash bag full of weed that belonged to her older brother John.

"Hey, why don't you give me a little bit of that weed?" I whisper in Jasmine's ear knowing that she would say no.

"You know I can't do that," Jasmine told me with a shocked look on her face. "How did you even know that it was weed in there anyway? I live here and never saw that much weed before in my life."

"I guess I have a nose for it," I told her. I had started smoking weed with Red and Money. "I respect you for saying no, which shows me that I could always trust you."

"Well, if you steal a pinch of it I will not say anything," she told me.

"No, I don't steal either," I told her while I thought about how much of a difference that trash bag could change my position in life. "Just make sure you tell him that I found it when I leave."

"Okay!" she told me happy that I wasn't a thief.

After that, it seemed like her brother started to like me even more. He would let me come over the house when their mother wasn't home, so since I no longer had to sneak around; their house became my little home away from home.

Still, I was homeless, and in the streets with only a gun. My brother and I would make sure each other was alright every night, but he was living with an older woman. I ran the streets 24/7: making money during the day and spending the night at Jasmine's house.

Although Red had cut me off, I still had my own customers. I would buy double ups from the neighborhood dealers with my customers' money, and then keep the money left over for myself.

Doing this helped me build up a lot of clientèle that would deal with me and only me because of my dedication to the streets. After I re-established myself as a hustler, and even though I was homeless, I put my money first. The whole hood adopted me as the son of the streets. All of my customers treated me like family and even called me "son."

I had mad love in the streets, and because of my own homeless experiences, I treated everybody with the utmost respect. I knew I was not better than anybody out there and that at any moment I could end up back at square one if I ever stopped hustling. People didn't understand why I gave so much respect to crack heads, but I knew that they had something that I did not; they had a home to go to at night. Even if that meant government funded housing, they had a home. I envied them for that, and needed them to survive off of. They were my life line.

## Chapter 10

On my 16th birthday Tyrone and I threw a North Side house party. One of Tyrone's customers let us pay his girlfriend Suds to use her basement to have the party. Tina Suds was a beautiful petite woman at the age of 32 years old; she was light skinned with long pretty hair. She wore glasses and had one open face gold tooth in her mouth, which gave her a down south flavor. She wasn't a crack head, but simply still with a man who went from being a big time dealer to a big time smoker after serving a 5 year prison bit. She did smoke weed though and got high from time to time by lacing a joint here or there, so we had to pay her money and give her boyfriend Brock some dope on top of that.

Suds lived on Elmer Street, which is the heart of the North Side. Since Elmer ran through Humboldt Street and all of the other major streets that ran through the North Side, Tyrone and I re-named Elmer Street the E- Way.

Everybody was at my party, but the person who shocked me the most was Charity. She was the girl from my dreams and my first love at first sight. Jasmine was also at the party wearing a short skirt and looking good, so I didn't get to spend too much time with Charity.

Charity was looking so good; she was fully developed in her daisy duke shorts, with long silky hair, an angelic face, and a smile that made the whole dark basement light up. We danced a few times and exchanged beeper numbers though. She was there with her boyfriend who was one of my homeboys from the hood, but still treated me like a long lost friend.

On top of paying for the party, Tyrone and I brought all kinds of liquor. The party was a blast, and after we showed even the grown folks a good time, we gained a lot of street credibility. Not only did I invite everybody from the hood; I also invited all of my loyal customers. I paid them to cook barbecue on the grill for everybody in the neighborhood, and let them and anybody else drink as much as they could.

Suds and I got really close that night. She started to call me her son too. Suds had three children of her own though, but her oldest daughter Sherrie and her son Das were incarcerated in the juvenile system. The only one of her children that lived at home with her was Pooh-Pooh who was only 11 years old.

Eventually, I asked Suds to let me use her house to set up shop. I promised to pay her $20 everyday plus help her pay the bills every month. Suds didn't care anything about the money and let me move in with her. And even though she didn't care about the money, I kept my word and paid her everyday like I promised. Suds loved me and taught me everything from how to cook up my own crack, to being a real hustler.

Immediately after I moved in, Suds put Brock out, and treated me like I was the man of the house. Suds used to sell drugs herself, so she knew everybody. My customer base increased drastically! I started to make and see serious money, and still kept the same attitude as before. I treated everybody with respect, so everybody loved me and still considered me "The son of the streets."

Not only did Suds hook me up with more customers, but she also knew all of the big time dealers who I could cop my drugs from. After the first couple of months there, Suds and I became very close to each other. I trusted her and treated her like my mother.

The drought came that next summer, and it was dry all over the city of South Bend. Nobody had any dope on the streets, so unless you knew the major dealers who copped in Chicago or Detroit, you had to pay extreme prices for bullshit. Luckily for me, Suds had all of the big time dealers in her back pocket. She practically raised all of them, so she kept me functioning and at a regular price so that I could tax everybody else that had no other choice but to deal with me.

I was the only person on the North Side with good dope, and since I wouldn't sell anybody big pieces, I had so much traffic coming in and out of Suds that the police would sit on the corner and watch all day long. We got smart though and just had a big barbecue everyday to mix the customers up with daisy dukes and belly shirts. Even the police couldn't resist the pretty young tenders and eventually, we had them too eating barbecue. The police turned from watching us to protection for us without even knowing it.

After Red had seen that I was hustling good he was trying his hardest to get me back on his team, but I was my own boss.

"If you want me to work under you again, you would have to give me all soft work. I cook up my own dope now, and I am copping an 8th of a key with my own money," I told Red at one of my weekend barbecue bashes that he and Money attended. "Can you do that and still throw me an additional 8th both for the same price?"

"Yeah, but do you think you can handle that much dope at once?" Red asked me underestimating me.

"What? I can handle a whole key," I told him feeling cocky and confident.

Red declined my offer, and not because he didn't believe I could handle it, but because the drought had effected his business too. At least that is what Money said, but Tyrone and I knew the real reason was that we were getting too big and coming up too fast for him to supply or even support our come up. Here we were the same little niggas that he was talking in parables to a year ago, and now we making moves. I went from homeless to a young figure in the streets over night. Thanks to Suds!

I continued to deal with this guy name O who was also from the West Side of town. He was cool, but he would always want to pick Tyrone and me up to go riding around with him. O was trying to be our friend, but I didn't need another friend, I needed a good connect. I was in no position to leave my block, because every time I would leave I would miss all sorts of money.

"I know you hungry for this money, but you need to enjoy yourself sometimes," O told me one day.

*The Son of the Streets...*
*Terrence leRoy Baker*

I wasn't trying to hear that shit. I needed to get paid. Eventually he would only pick up Tyrone. At first I used to get jealous too, but I was cool with the fact that while Tyrone ran around with O, I was getting his money and my money too. I knew better than to get comfortable, because in the back of my mind I knew that if my own mother turned me away to the streets, that the streets, Suds, and all of my customers would turn there backs on me too the moment I get too comfortable. I couldn't have that! So I worked Monday to Monday, 24/7. I was making doctor money at the age of 16, and knew one day that I would be on top of the game: at least that is what I thought.

## **Chapter 11**

That summer of 1996, was the climax of my career. With the drought still in effect, and being the only guys on the North Side who stayed consistently with dope, we came up a lot.

Not only were we making our money, but we were also making everybody else's too, which brought a lot of jealousy and hate along with our good fortune. Still, we were young, so we were flashy with our money, buying all sorts of unnecessary bullshit. We had all of the latest pagers, the latest Jordan's, and dressed to kill everyday.

At the end of the summer O was going to his family reunion up in Saginaw, Michigan. He asked us both to come with him, but I quickly rejected his offer.

"I knew you wouldn't stop hustling for a whole weekend anyway," O told me out of the blue.

"Am I supposed to stop hustling, or would it benefit me more if I hustled even harder?" I asked him offended.

"Why don't you leave your beeper here with me Tyrone? I would hate to see all of that good money going to waste," I told Tyrone knowing that he would choose the vacation over hard work and dedication.

"Please, all of my people already know where to come if I aint around anyway," Tyrone joked and we all started laughing.

O, seen the opportunity as a way for him to keep his people happy too, so he offered me to keep his beeper too. Then he left me a half of a key of already cooked cocaine on top of that. I immediately came to the realization that he had this all planned out from the beginning, but still, I didn't object to his offer. I knew that with three pumping pagers, and all of that dope; that I would immediately be on a whole other level by the time they returned. On top of that, I would have access to not only Tyrone's customers, but O's too; which I could recruit onto my team until I come up and cut him off.

Everything was about planning from that point on. Tyrone and O were leaving on Thursday night, so we all hooked up that morning and got everything situated. Then I had Suds rent me a brand new Cadillac from Avis rentals. I figured if I was going to be moving around good, I might as well be riding in style too.

I went and picked up my girl, and we rode around all night getting money. All of our customers were mesmerized by the car and the way I was rolling. Eventually, I built up a business relationship with O's people, and was considered in charge because of the amount of weight he left with me to move for him.

By Friday night I had moved all of my dope and O's half of a key. Jasmine and I decided to rent a suite downtown at the Marriott hotel where we sat up and counted out $21,500. I owed O $10,000, but that still left me with almost $12,000. I had always maintained $2,000 to $3,000 and would still have to use Tyrone's money with mines to cop, but now I had more money by myself than both of us put together.

Still, my problem wasn't the fact that I had all of this money, but they wouldn't be back in town for two more days, and all of our beepers were still going crazy with business. What I needed was a quick connect, and with it being dry, that meant I only had a couple options.

"What's wrong with you?" Jasmine asked me.

"I am in a bind. All of this money and I don't have any more product to sell to my people," I told her trying to sound like a big shot.

"You want me to call my brother for you?" she asked me trying to help out as much as she could.

"Your brother only sells weed," I told her not trying to involve her in the middle of my business at first.

"You don't know that," she said picking up the phone in the suite to call.

"What did he say?" I asked after she hung up the phone after about a minute.

"He said to come by there tomorrow," she said in a nonchalant way.

Surely he already knew what I wanted. He had seen me rolling up out of the driveway of his mother's house in the Cadillac. I figured I could call it a night and turned off all of the pagers so that I could shift my focus on Jasmine. We went out to eat, then to the movies.

That night was special, because it was like we were a team. Once we got back to the hotel we were both tipsy from the wine we drank at Red Lobster. The waiter was one of my good customers, so he looked out for us. I was high off of the hydro weed I had been smoking all day long, but Jasmine didn't smoke so she was the driver.

After we got out of the shower together we decided to make use of the heart shaped Jacuzzi in the middle of the room.

"No need to waste a good room," Jasmine said to me while she filled up the tub with bubbles and water.

"Say it ain't so!" I joked while I rolled up another blunt of hydro.

Once I dimmed the lights and turned on the clock radio, I joined her inside the boiling hot water. Immediately she started to rub all over me in all of the right places and kissing me on my chest. Sitting back like a king smoking on my blunt, I thought about my life for a split second. Then after snapping back into reality, I gave her my blunt and made her take a hit. She choked uncontrollably! I started by kissing her sensitive neck, then I made my way down to her perfectly firm and fully developed breasts. While sucking on her nipples I was stroking her insides with my long fingers getting her body ready for my love tool.

For some reason tonight was different. I felt in control as if I was on top of the world. I lifted her up onto the side of the Jacuzzi and while still playing with her sex nest, I started kissing and licking down her belly; sending her into frenzy.

On my knees still inside of the water, with only her legs inside of the water with me, I made my way to her fantasies. Once I got down to her thighs she was anticipating my tongue so much that she started to cum in a stream of liquid all over my face before I ever even made contact. We were both inexperienced to the oral pleasures of sex, but still I kissed her lips down there as if they were her mouth. Then I slowly eased my tongue inside and around her clit like I was giving her a French kiss. She came uncontrollable time after time.

"Oh my God nothing has ever felt this good to me before," Jasmine screamed to me over the sound of the bubbles in the Jacuzzi.

"You like that," I said with my face still buried inside of her.

"Yes! Please don't stop! Please!"

Then after she almost fell over the side of the tub, I helped her to her feet. As I was getting out of the water I was exposing my rock hard sausage meat. In her eyes all I could see was hunger.

She dropped down to her knees and took me deep enough into her throat to choke. I slowly helped her position her neck so that she could accomplish the ultimate goal: my climax. She took to it like a duck to water, and before I knew it, I was blasting, releasing a big load of stress off of my chest onto hers.

## **Chapter 12**

That next day was everything I had expected it to be. John was already at their mother's house when we arrived. As soon as we got out of the car he was outside ready to discuss business with me. It was kind of weird, because of the fact that Jasmine had just spent the night with me. I felt like he was her father ready to scold me about his daughter. However, that wasn't the case.

"What's up, Terry?" he asked me.

"Oh, nothing much, I just wanted to know if you could do me a favor," I replied as Jasmine made her way inside the house, leaving us two alone to talk.

"What kind of favor, doing what?" John asked confused.

"I don't know how to ask you, but I need some cocaine. You see my regular connection is out of town for the weekend."

"I'm sorry, but I don't fool around with that shit! Maybe I could hook you up with some pounds of weed, but that is about it. Why, how much of your own money do you have?" he asked me.

"About $11, 000," I explained.

"You doing pretty good I see; however, I would've called my Mexican friend for you, but he only deals with a whole key or more at a time," John explained.

"How much would he charge me for a whole key?" I asked aware of the fact that I did have enough money if I used O's money to make a quick flip.

"I don't know, but I am positive that it will be more than $11, 000," he explained.

"Well, actually, I have more than that, but just didn't want to spend it all at once," I lied not wanting to tell him the truth about where the other money was coming from.

"I will tell you what. Do you mind if I take your rental around to his house?" he asked.

"Not at all," I said eager to show his friend I meant business.

After John left me to go handle our business, I went inside the house. Jasmine was upstairs about to take a shower and get dressed, so I went down in the basement where her mother was watching television and smoking a joint at.

Jasmine's mother always did like me. She would smoke a joint with me from time to time and talk shit to me about her daughter, using protection if we ever become sexually active, and getting a job. Jasmine's uncle was also there. His name was Chuck, but he never spoke to me; however, I would always go out of my way to speak to him. He was cool: had all of the nicest cars; and dressed like a straight up pimp. Not to mention the fact that he had one of the finest women I had ever seen before in my life. Her name was Dee. They all were from California, and acted like it too.

This day in particular was different; he offered for me to hit the joint, already aware of the fact that I smoked with his sister. I quickly accepted and after hitting it, I offered to roll up some of my own hydro weed as well.

We smoked a few joints, so I was high as a kite when Jasmine came back downstairs.

"I thought that you were gone with John," she said surprised to see me still there with the car gone.

"No, I've been down here just chilling," I said like I was a member of the family.

"Yeah, I can see that, and you look like you can't see anything through those eyes of yours. They so red and tight that I thought you were Chinese when I walked down here," she said with sarcasm.

Then John pulled back up into the driveway blasting Tupac's 'All eyes on me' CD in my rental, so I went back outside to meet him.

"He said he could sell you a key for $19, 000, but you would have to give me the money to take to him up front. Actually, that is a great price considering that the drought is still barely in effect. Can you come up with that much money?" he asked.

"Can I? The money is already in the trunk of the car!"

"What? You mean to tell me that you had me flying around with that much money in this car?" John yelled obviously upset.

"Yeah, but it is hidden real well. Let me show you," I said protectively.

"I told you so!" I said after removing the spare tire in the trunk.

"I thought you said you only had $11, 000?" John inquired in a concerned way.

"That's not all I have, just all I wanted to spend," I lied to him.

I took out $2, 500 then gave him the bag it was in. John just looked at me as if it were blood money; then he left. I went back inside the house to where Jasmine was in the kitchen waiting for me.

"So, what's up?" she asked.

"Everything is looking good and guess what else?"

"What?" she asked.

"I am taking you shopping," I said smiling and wrapping my arms around her.

"Take me shopping for what? I don't need any clothes. You the one who need to get something to wear," she said kissing me in a teasing way.

"You know that is what I love about you, you never think of yourself first," I whispered to her in between kisses.

"I tell you what, we can go shopping some other time, because I already have plenty of brand new outfits at Suds' house," I explained. "Soon as John gets back, we will go over there to pick me up some clothes, then we can go back to the room after I handle my business so that I can get dressed and wash you up off of me."

"OK!" she said in a sensual voice ready to get her morning dose of my loving.

John returned after about 20 minutes had passed. He blew the horn for me. I had already turned all of the beepers back on, and they all were banging, so I was ready to go.

I got into the passenger seat of the rental, and on the floor was a big block wrapped in yellow tape the size of a brick. Even though I had been selling dope for a while, I had never seen a wrapped up key before. I was amazed.

Along with the yellow tape it was wrapped in, it was rectangular in shape, and had a small slit in the middle of it over a Lexus stamp that was engraved in it. I peeked into the opening and couldn't see anything other than some fish scale, shiny cocaine. I was impressed!

## The Son of the Streets...
### Terrence leRoy Baker

After I got everything situated with John, Jasmine and I headed toward the North Side to Suds' house. To my surprise, her daughter Sherrie was at home for a weekend pass from her facility. Sherrie was a chocolate wonder: a dark skinned goddess; with really long silky hair; a body like a coke bottle; and an intimidating presence that would make any women nervous with her around their man.

Sherrie was a fast girl coming up, involving herself with the older crowd, and dating all of the older dope dealers around the neighborhood. She was in girl school because she claimed some cocaine that the police found in the car after pulling her and her boyfriend Amp over.

I had known Sherrie growing up in the neighborhood, but she always called me a Rudy Pooh. She considered me a lame, because I never carried myself like a gangster, even though I hung around the same crowd as the gangsters she admired so much. I still used to flirt with her, hoping that I could join the number of North Side thugs, both young and old, who made their way inside of her pants. Deep down I knew she always had a crush on me too, but what I didn't know was that I would one day live in her house and sleep inside of her bed. Tables sure turn around.

Now as she seen me pulling up in the front of her mother's house in my Cadillac rental, she began to get wet in-between her legs.

"What's up Rudy Pooh?" Sherrie asked me in an amazed sort of voice thinking that I was stopping by to speak to her.

"Nothing," I said passing her to enter the house that I had made my home over the last year.

Suds immediately introduced us to each other like we didn't know each other already. Then she explained to her daughter that I had been staying there, and that all of the clothes in her bedroom closet belonged to me. I spoke to her then went into our bedroom that I had made my own over the time to go to my safe that I kept on the floor beside the bed.

Sherrie came into the room just as I was locking up my safe after first arguing with her mother about me staying there.

"Look Rudy Pooh, I've been locked up for six months, and that means that I aint had no dick, so unless you drop that bitch off in your car and come pick me up, then you can expect me to be having some company in our room tonight. Shit, I would've fucked someone last night up in here, but I got too drunk to stay up until Momma went out," she said nodding at my safe on the floor.

"You know, that sounds like a great offer, but I will have to pass on it. And another thing, I am not your damn Rudy Pooh, and I really don't give a fuck who you fuck up in here. As you can see, I am not hurting for any desperate pussy," I said to her in a way like I would fuck her, but when I felt like it.

"Well then," she said even more turned on by me now than ever, and walked up to me and grabbed my dick through my pants.

"I guess I will just have to wait until you make time for me, but in the mean time," she said to me in a seductive way noticing my arousal. Then she kissed me on my cheek and turned around to leave the room with me standing there hard as a rock. "See you soon!"

After getting everything that I needed for the night, as far as my scale, Pyrex, and clothes, I left. I didn't leave the brick in the safe though. Even though I had been staying there for a while, I still didn't want Sud or her crazy ass daughter to know that I had that much cocaine at all, better yet in the house. So I decided to cook it up in the microwave in my room.

I gave Suds some money, and told her I loved her like I always did before leaving the house. She loved me too, and called me "Son" before letting me go. I told her the room number at my hotel.

Suds was like a real street mother to me, she would support me no matter what, and tell me about myself if I ever got beside myself. People forget how important that is growing up, but after my mother turned her back on me, I came to the realization that without someone to keep me in line, I wouldn't of been able to make it on my own in the streets without somebody else to respect other than myself.

The funny thing about the way she treated me was that she treated me like a man. She taught me how to take care of home first, and the responsibility of paying bills and grocery shopping. With her help, I still grew up fast, but complete;

other than cleaning up after myself, but that is
another story in its self. Besides, nobody is perfect.

## Chapter 13

Once I got back into the car, Jasmine was looking at me almost disturbed, but more so ready to leave from in front of the house. Even though I was staying at Suds' house, Jasmine never would come inside. She always thought Suds and I had something going on more than what it seemed from the outside. But, she, like so many others who thought the same thing, was wrong.

"Why was that girl just staring at me, and who is she?" she asked me after we pulled away from the house.

"Oh, that's Sherrie, Suds daughter. Don't worry about her, because she isn't talking about anything," I said.

"Shit, how can I ignore somebody when they looking all at me with jealousy and hate in they eyes?"

"I seriously doubt if she is jealous or hates you. Maybe you got the wrong impression," I tried to explain.

"Nigga please! I am a female, so trust and believe that I know another bitch better than anyone of you niggas do because all ya'll think with is your dicks; so don't even try to play me," Jasmine said snapping on me.

I just left it at that. There was no need in
going into a battle that I knew I can't win, even if I
was right. Which I knew I wasn't!

We got to the room, and Jasmine ordered us
some room service. I was preoccupied with my
beepers and phone in the room. So far I had 11
ounces set up to be sold at $900 each. Some were
hard, but some were soft and those went for $1,000.
All together there is 36 ounces in a key, so after I
handled the business for the day, I would be able to
take care of O when he returned. Then with the
extras, I will still have 25 ounces or so left for
myself, which would be about three quarters of a
key: plenty of dope to make enough money to cop
my own key with. Also, this meant that I wouldn't
be dealing with O or Red anymore. I now had a
better connect than them both; and with the drought
in effect, I could take the streets.

I made sure to inform all of O's clientèle
that I would be doing my own thing from now on,
which I was sure they could tell because my dope
was better, different, and I was selling both hard
and soft. Not to mention the fact that O was still out
of town, so they knew it didn't come from him. I
gave all of his people my cell phone number since
they all wanted weight so that they could contact
me directly. However, I kept my people on my
pager number: except for the loyal ones who spent
big.

I knew what I was doing was wrong, but I
was young and thirsty for that money, shit, O said
so himself. It was all coming naturally to me. I was
taking over the streets one ounce at a time, and with
the help of the feds being in town causing a
drought, I had an opportunity to capitalize on a

power move and took it. The game is all about timing, so when your time to shine presents itself, you take it and run with it at whatever price it takes. Tomorrow isn't promised in the dope game, and who is to say that staying loyal to, or under somebody is promising for your future either. It is about ambition and persistence, and I was making power moves with that in mind.

That weekend changed me and everything around me forever. I was now on the same level as the people who I looked up to, and I can't say it didn't go to my head, but I still stayed true to the game. However, the thing about the game that most people fail to realize is that any and everything goes.

So, with that in mind I took care of everything lined up for the day, then I got dressed up; it was a Saturday night. I had a pocket full of money; a brand new rental car; and, a bad ass chick on my side that was actually making my street dreams possible for me.

Jasmine had to go to work the next morning and was cool with me hanging out in the streets. So, after we made love, or should I say had sex a time or two, I dropped her off at home promising to pick her up from work the next day.

John was in the parking lot, so after Jasmine got out of the car he got in.

"How was it?" he asked with a mysterious smile on his face.

"Great, I was wondering if we could do it again after I finished this one. It will probably be about a week or so though," I explained.

"Actually, that is what I wanted to talk to you about," he replied to my proposition. "I was wondering if you could move some of these pounds of weed for me too. I really ain't tripping about the dope, I will hook you up on that. But, I can use your help pushing some of this weed in return. I can front them to you 10 at a time for about $650 a piece. It is some good shit too; you could probably get $900-$1,000 a piece on the streets."

"That is cool, because my whole hood is looking for weed. I thought about coming at you about it before when I found those pounds in the basement," I said showing my loyalty.

"Yeah, Jasmine told me about that. I knew then that you could be trusted and was a cool little dude. That was almost a year ago, and boy you came a long way since then. Tell you what, my uncle Chuck is supposed to get some keys from Cali, he already knows about you, so he said he will put you down. Don't say nothing to him about it thought. I am sure he is waiting until they hit here before talking to you. If you need another key before then, I will hook you up with my Mexican, but if you can wait until Unc gets on, I am sure the price will be a lot cheaper," he explained.

"I'll see what I can do. When will you be ready for me on the trees?" I asked.

"Come by here tomorrow around six. I will have them here waiting for you."

80

"Bet, I am picking Jasmine up from work tomorrow anyway, so I will be here," I mentioned while checking my pager that was peeping non-stop.

After leaving Jasmine's house I headed over to the West Side where Money was waiting on me. He was over Red's crib when I pulled up in front of his house, so I parked and walked down the street instead of driving.

I was already fresh to death with the Jordan's and matching Ice Berg sweat suit. I felt like me pulling up in front of Red's house in my rental would be violating the first of the 48 Laws of Power: "Never outshine the Master." Besides, even though I had came up, I still considered Red and Money the people who got my feet wet in the game, so they both had my utmost respect.

"What's up big timer," Red said sarcastically. "Word on the streets is that you handling all of O's business."

"Yeah, he went out of town for the weekend and left me with his beeper. Shit most of his business was taken care of the first day though. Since then I've been doing my own thing.

"Listen to little Tea! So, you handling your own thing now, ha? Well it sure must be nice. Looks like you doing real good too. Money tells me you got a cell phone and shit," he said. I knew he wasn't too happy with me. "Why didn't you give me your new number? You do know you still my favorite North Sider? Don't you?"

"I still got the same beeper number," I said while writing down my cell number for him.

"You ready to roll out?" Money asked.

"Yeah, I am waiting for you," I said throwing him the car keys. "Why don't you drive? You the original Cadillac pimp if I remember correctly."

"I got you, but I need to make a couple of runs: one out South; and one out East," he explained. "What you doing in this sweet ass Caddy anyway? You know this is my style!"

"It's a rental. Suds got it for me for a week," I explained referring to the cream color Seville with the custom chrome Cadillac rims to match. "Besides, it was either this or a Buick."

"You made the right choice! This muthafucka is tight," Money said as he smashed on the gas pulling us down the block past Red who was just smiling at his protégés.

We rode around for a while handling a little business. I made a couple of runs to my room and over to Suds house. Money was handling his business in between mine.

I had to meet one of my loyal customers over Suds, and I was going to make this my last stop of the night, but when we got over Suds house she wasn't home and my customer hadn't yet arrived. However, it was still a car out front. Not thinking about it, I walked on in the house to find

## The Son of the Streets...
### Terrence leRoy Baker

Sherrie was having a little get together. The music was blasting and one of Sherrie's friends who only knew me by Rudy Pooh saw me and yelled for her.

"Sherrie, Rudy Pooh is here!"

Sherrie never responded, and I wasn't waiting for one either. All I could think about is the fact that our bedroom door was closed. I was about to go in there, but first I cut down the music.

"What are you doing?" Trice, one of Sherrie's friends yelled at me.

Sherrie came running up out of the room looking like she thought her mother had raided the little party. She looked all messed up: her clothes were barely on right; her hair was all over her head; and if it wasn't for the fact that she was sweating up a storm, I would've thought she was asleep.

"Oh, girl that ain't nobody but Tea," she told her friend. "Bitch you done messed up my nut! You know I ain't had no dick in over a year!"

"Girl, you never told me that Rudy Pooh was Tea. I would've thought that he was fuckable the way you were talking," Trice said.

"Thanks for the compliment, but I wouldn't fuck your fat ass with a dildo anyway, so don't you worry about me. Besides, it looks like I was only one minute too late to fuck you, ain't that right?" I said to Sherrie in a jealous and betrayed feeling sort of way.

Sherrie just stood there looking busted and like she done lost her only chance to make me look at her any other way but like a whore. You never get a second chance to make a first impression!

"So, who is in our room honey?" I said with some sarcasm.

"Nobody and do me a favor and please don't tell Momma," she pleaded to me

"What the fuck do I look like to you the police? Look, I am about to go out tonight, so I need to get something out of there. Could you get rid of your little company? If you do I will take you and little Mrs. Piggy over there with me," I proposed.

"Let me talk to you real fast first in Momma's room," she whispered into my ear.

We stepped into her Momma's room and immediately after closing the door, Sherrie started to try to explain herself to me like she had betrayed her husband or worse.

"I was with Amp. He is my ex-boyfriend, but look, I don't want him to see you, so please leave and come back in fifteen minutes," she begged me.

"Cool, but somebody is on there way here to meet me, so I will be out front in the car waiting for them," I told her heading for the bedroom door.

Sherrie stopped me and reached down into my sweat suit grabbing my hard dick. I was for some reason getting turned on by the whole situation. She smirked at me noticing my erection and in one swift motion dropped down on her knees and took me into her mouth. She went to work on me slow but yet strong and accurately, causing me to explode in her mouth in mere seconds. She still never quit until the last drop of my liquid love was down her throat heading towards her heart.

After swallowing me up, Sherrie got up and kissed me on the cheek. Then she left the room before I could focus on the moment. All I could think about is how she probably was kissing that nigga with my nut all in her mouth.

When I came out of the room, I not only felt guilty, but I also felt sticky and nasty. Nobody was in the house except Sherrie and her boyfriend who was locked inside the room. The music wasn't playing anymore either. Then my customer knocked on the open door and let himself in.

"What is up Mr. Tea?" Boss Bob asked as he walked in the house.

"Waiting on you," I said after giving him a hug and some dap.

"Shit, I've been outside with Money for a good ten minutes. He is out there with five girls in your Caddy chilling. Maybe I should leave you alone and start messing with him. It looks like he the one with all the women," he joked to me.

"Them girls is Sherrie's friends, Suds daughter Sherrie is here for the weekend," I explained briefly.

"Oh yeah, what she look like? Is she as fine as her mother?" Bob asked joking.

"I don't know, but I do know she too young for your old ass. You wouldn't know what to do with her fast ass," I joked back.

"Oh, and I guess you got jokes. I bet I could do more for them young girls then you or Money put together, shit. Ya'll still too wet behind the ear to know how to please a women. Once I put my old school tongue game down, they wouldn't want to look at you young niggas again."

"You probably right! You probably right!" I said as I counted his money to find it was short.

"Well, I will call you tomorrow," Bob said making a swift exit knowing I was counting his money.

I let him go anyway, but will just short him next time he calls me. I always get even money, sometimes even if I had to get it the hard way.

## Chapter 14

Back outside, Money was sitting in the back seat of the car now, and one of Sherrie's friends was in the back seat with him. They were talking as if they knew one another. Everybody knew Money, he was like a ghetto celebrity coming up: from all of the different cars he drove, the clothes he was wearing, he was know for having money since middle school. Trice and this other quiet girl named Mya was in the driver and passenger seats. Tiffany was the one in the back with Money.

I walked up to the passenger side window where Mya was and knocked lightly scaring everybody in the car including Money half to death. I always had a thing for Mya. We went to school together, so I used to flirt with her, but nothing serious.

Mya was short, but thick as a brick; she had some beautiful hazel eyes; some long hair that she kept done; and was very smart in school, so she had that innocent look about herself.

"May I help you," she asked me still startled.

"Sure, you could start by turning down the music, and then you can let me hit the blunt," I said motioning to the blunt in her hand.

"Do you want to sit in the car? You know how the police be sitting on the corner all the time around here," she asked probably not even aware that the car was mine in the first place; either that or just wanting me to sit next to her. However, I took her offer and got into the front seat with her. She immediately got up on top of my lap.

"I didn't even know that you smoked weed Rudy Pooh!" Trice said to me passing me the blunt.

"Yeah, I smoke miss piggy!"

Everyone in the car started laughing. Meanwhile, Mya on the other hand was getting comfortable on my lap. Even though I was Ice Berg down, I didn't mind one bit. As a matter of fact, I didn't want her to ever get up off of me, and she never did.

Trice asked Money if she could drive around the block; Money immediately told her to ask me. I answered her question before she could even open her mouth. I told her to drive up to Frankie's Barbecue spot out West, and to be careful. I had better things to worry about, like the bad chick sitting on my lap exchanging shotguns from the blunt. I was holding on to Mya like she was an infant child, and even though she wasn't I treated her like my women, even if only for one night.

When we got to Frankie's, it was jam packed. Everybody was out stunting in there whips. I sent Trice inside to get everybody in the car rib tip dinners, and I even got Sherrie one too. Trice didn't mind, because all she talked about since I mentioned Frankie's was if I was going to buy her a meal. Mya was having the time of her life, and all of us were high as a kite.

As soon as Trice got the food she got in the back seat of the car messing up Mya and my mood;

changing the driving situation meant one of us
needed to drive. However, Trice was quiet as a
mouse and showing me the utmost respect from that
moment on. And they say money can't buy you
love; they must not know how much love a rib tip
dinner from Frankie's can get you. I was no longer
Rudy Pooh in her eyes, from that moment on I was
Tea. Still, to me, she will always be Mrs. Piggy. I
guess life is just funny like that, to get respect you
got to earn it.

Money got into the drivers seat, so I jumped
in the back where Mya followed me. Tiffany
jumped in the front with him. Mya made herself
back at home in my arms again, but this time, laying
her whole body on mine like we were together and
nothing or nobody else mattered.

Trice lived on the South Side, so when
Money made his way over there to handle some
business, she suggested we drop her off. Being that
she was full and in the way, I agreed jokingly. But
to gain her loyalty, I offered her Sherrie's rib tip
dinner. She knew what I wanted from her in return,
and even if I would've never given her Sherrie's
meal, she still probably wouldn't have said anything
to her about the way Mya was all over me. Actually,
I didn't care if she told her of not, but, just that she
didn't make it the first priority on her list to do once
she got in the house. I was sure Mya felt the same
way too.

After Trice said her good byes, we all
headed down to my suite at the Marriott. There
wasn't much to talk about, so I just let the music
and weed do all the rest of the conversations for us.
Mya had her hand on my leg as to show me that I
could have her any and every way that I wished,

and Money and Tiffany were getting better acquainted by the second. I was sure they had already sealed the deal as well.

Once we got into the parking garage at the hotel, they both started asking each other lame questions the way girls always do when it is about to go down orgy style, as to let each other know it was up to them to stay or leave. Most girls lie about their sex life, so when their friends witness them on some flip shit, they either feel uncomfortable or get even more turned on. They choose to stay, lucky for us!

I immediately took control of their insecurity. I assured them that it would only be a minute and that they can simply come inside to eat their food and that after I took care of my business we would leave. However, I failed to mention to them that they were my business.

As soon as we got inside of the suite they were both amazed and immediately made themselves at home. The suite was set up in two separate rooms, with the front room having a couch that let out into a bed; and a jacuzzi in the middle of the floor. Also the master bedroom had a king size bed with mirrors on the ceiling and wall around the bed for extended vision during sexual endeavors.

"Oh, can I get up in the jacuzzi?" Mya asked.

"Sure! As long as I can join you," I said.

"I want to too, but I don't want to mess up my hair," Tiffany said.

"That is cool, because I ain't getting up in there either, so we can go in the back room and watch a movie," Money suggested to her.

They went back into the room; I ordered us all some champagne while we waited for the water to fill up. Then rolled up two blunts, one for us and one for them.

Mya was in the bathroom, and had been in there for over ten minutes before she came out with a hotel robe on.

"I didn't have anything else to wear, so I am going to get in naked. Can you handle that?" she asked me.

"Can I? I wouldn't want it any other way," I said after adding some bubbles to the water before activating the system.

Just as I finished fixing up the tub, room service knocked at the door. He was the same guy as the night before, so there was no problem getting the alcohol. I tipped him $10 as always, and came back into the room to find Mya already in the Jacuzzi. I just smiled.

"Money, I got the drinks," I yelled. However, he never answered so I took that as a good signal.

I went on and made Mya and I some glasses of the Moet, and then got undressed right there in front of her. She was looking at me like I was either crazy or sexy, which ever one didn't matter to me, as I got into the hot water. She immediately got in

91

between my legs and cuddled up in my arms where she felt safe.

After handing her a glass of champagne, I lit up the blunt that was in the ashtray on the ledge of the tub. She took a big gulp killing it all and sat it down. I sipped on mine and then followed her lead. Then I put the blunt down after giving her one last shot gun. She was playing in the water with my already hard dick.

"You don't waste any time I see?" I asked her as I too put my hand on her fat juicy pussy.

"Why should I?"

"Well for one, if you keep playing with me, you might find it hard to stop. Some call me ad-dick-tive."

"How do you know I want to stop?" she asked me while jacking me off.

Next thing I knew she was lifting up so that I could easily slide my yearning member inside of her inviting haven. All I could think about was how I didn't have on a condom, and how good it felt inside of her. Knowing how water and latex didn't mix anyway, I quickly pushed that safe thought to the back of my mind, and sat back and enjoyed the ride.

She was taking it slow, making me feel her every move, and she was squeezing me tight with her muscles in between her legs to assure that I didn't slip and fall out. Seeing that she couldn't take too much of me, I exploited her weakness by pumping back from the bottom to make sure that she got every inch of my love tool. It was her who felt so obligated to have me raw, so I was giving it to her. Before I knew it I was filling her up with my seed. She was already use to me by then, so once she felt me coming, she put all of her weight down on me as to accept my very seed into her life.

After our first session we sat back and just chilled. We finished our drinks and smoked our blunt up. I was feeling both guilty and good at the same time. I was sure she felt the same way too. I had a girlfriend and was quite sure that she had a man too. She was too gorgeous not to. I was sure of it, but could've cared less. We went for round two.

## **Chapter 15**

The next morning Money and I dropped them off at Tiffany's house. I exchanged phone numbers with Mya and we hugged and kissed. She hugged me real strong.

"You were great last night," she told me while still holding on for dear life in a way a woman does to show a man that they don't want to become another statistic of the one night stand.

"Thanks! You weren't too bad yourself," I joked.

"When can I see you again?" she asked me.

"Maybe we could hook up next weekend. Call me!" I told her before leaving her where she stood on the curb.

"I can't wait!" she told me while leaning into the passenger window where I was sitting and kissing me passionately for the first time.

It was a Sunday morning, and I had a lot of things to do for the day. Money and I started our day off with breakfast at Lincoln Way Grill: the best breakfast spot in the city.

"So what is really going on?" Money asked me.

"I'm just chilling! Man I had a ball last night," I said.

"Fuck last night, I am talking about the suite, the rental, and shit, you dressed like you done just hit the lottery. It seems like just yesterday I was showing you how to weigh up twenties, and now you look like you could teach me a thing or two," money said with sarcasm.

"Nah, I just got a lucky break and took it. Shit, you know how hard it has been for your boy for the last year or so. I am out here all the way in the trenches of these streets. I might as well take the game to a whole new level; either that or get swallowed up by the vultures and snakes. There are two kinds of people in this world: predators and the prey. I feel like I must attack like a predator and the streets is my prey."

"I am feeling you on that, and I like to see my guy doing his own thing; but, just don't leave me out in the cold. Let me in on that good money you getting," Money said, and I could tell he was really feeling left out.

"Shit, you would be surprised how much has changed for me in just one week. I've been getting not only my money, but also O's and Tyrone's too."

"How you been doing that with them out of town and not to mention it's still drought season?" Money asked.

"Exactly. Remember I said I got a lucky break?"

"Yeah, but how?" he asked.

"Well once O's dope ran out, I went to Jasmine's brother and he hooked me up with a new Mexican connection, so I used all of our money to cop something big. Then I gave all of O's clientèle my new cell phone number and they've been calling me non-stop ever since," I explained not yet understanding completely the rules of silence.

"Man, you on some dirty shit, but I like it," Money said laughing through a mouth full of his ham and cheese omelet.

"Still, the Mexican's price is way cheaper; his shit is way better; and, he is still plentiful in the drought," I explained while stuffing my face with my custom made Colonial Burger on Texas toast.

"So, either way, you would've cut O off, but you needed his money to make it all work out to your advantage?" Money asked me.

"Close, but not yet the cigar," I said. "You are feeling me though."

"I was feeling you from the jump," Money corrected me, and I knew he meant more by that statement than what was on the surface. "So what are you going to tell O when he gets back today?"

"I ain't going to tell him shit! Hopefully, he will respect the game."

"Well look, Red is all out of dope too, so maybe you could hook him up with your Mexican connect," Money suggested.

"Nah, I ain't hooking nobody up with my connection. If he or anybody else needs some work, they going to have to call me, and I will middle man. One small problem though, he only deals in whole keys or better."

"So, you on some real coming up shit I see. How much he charging for a brick?" he asked me.

"I am charging Michael Jordan: $23, 000," I said in a correcting way knowing that it was a good price considering.

We finished off our morning with a fresh blunt of hydro. I dropped Money off and went over Suds house to drop off my clothes and things from the hotel room. Before I got dressed and finished putting things away, Tyrone paged me.

Suds was gone to drop Sherrie off in the rental, so I waited to call back. Sherrie had called herself washing all of my dirty clothes for me and the sheets off the bed. I guess she was trying to show me she was a good girl deep down inside.

"Tea, where you been at all weekend? I haven't seen my son in two days. You just have been running in and out of here like you don't love me anymore. Shit at least you used to eat dinner or breakfast with me," Suds yelled coming in the door.

"Oh, Suds, you know you will always be the most important women in my life. How could I stop loving you?" I told her playing along with her game, which usually is played before she asked for some money.

"Well you sure don't act like it!"

"I am sorry, I just been busy running nowhere fast," I said.

"You hungry?" she asked putting the icing on the cake.

"Naw, I just ate, but thank you."

"Good, because I really didn't feel like cooking anyway," she said with an attitude. "Tea, I need to take Pooh Pooh school shopping, and since today is such a beautiful day, I figured I would drive up to the Michigan City outlet."

"You know I already told Pooh I would take her shopping, so what else is it?" I asked knowing something else was cooking.

"Well, I wanted to drive in the Caddy. You been having all of the fun without me. So, I figured that the real women in your life should be driving your car since you put it in her name anyway," Suds said putting me in no position to say no.

"Sure, I need to go handle some business first," I told her.

"Tea, don't be spinning me on no bull shit like you do everybody else," Suds demanded.

"I got you honey!" I said as I kissed her on the cheek.

"You better have me!" Suds said in a flirtatious way.

"Stop playing with me woman before I have to prove that I am the man of this house," I played back. We always played these little games with each other when we were home alone.

Suds loved me and I loved her too. I'll would be 17 in a couple of days, and already knew what it felt like to be a man. Suds taught me that, and sometimes I cared about her in more ways than one. I always wondered if she felt the same way about me sometimes. As a matter of fact I am sure she did; however, those feelings may stay bottled up forever.

She was like a woman, friend, and mother to me mixed in one. The only time that I would realize that she was a lady was when she asked me for money. I guess that all comes from realizing that I am taking care of her. But, I would always snap out of it and come back to my senses. She was taking care of me too, and she has been from day one: she took me from boy to man mentally. Yeah, I had a natural crush on her, and of course she knew it, but feelings are something uncontrollable.

I always wondered if I was attached to Suds simply because of the fact that my mother gave up hope for me at such a young age. Suds accepted me for me, and as long as I was providing help to her, she would go to bat for me no matter what: I loved her for that and always will.

Life on the streets moves so fast that once you look back, a month or year has moved past. Either you are still doing the same thing; or, you could've fell off or came up. That roller coaster ride is what defines a true hustler, because you are going to fall off; but, what really matters is if you can learn from your mistakes and come back up even further than before.

## **Chapter 16**

On the way to go pick Jasmine up from work, I called Tyrone back from my cell phone.

"What is up my nigga?"

"Shit, what took you so long to call me back muthafucka. Nigga, don't be having me waiting on you like I am one of your hoes," Tyrone told me in a way that only he feels comfortable enough with me to talk to me in. Him and my brother, that is.

"Nigga, you already know that I am a one woman man, so are you calling my girl a hoe?" I asked.

"Oh, you with the wifey?" he whispered into the phone.

"Don't get all quiet now nigga. What's up with all that hoe shit you were just talking?" I asked again.

"Man you tripping, I called you a hoe ass nigga!" he lied.

"Oh, you can't try to fix that shit up now!"

"I'm sorry! Tell her I am sorry!" he pleads.

"Listen to your soft ass. I ain't even with her right now, but I am on my way to pick her up from work," I said laughing my heart out.

"You a fag, why you play so fucking much," Tyrone said not finding anything funny.

"So, how was your little vacation?" I asked him.

"What? Don't even try to play me. You know that nigga O had me up there on some bullshit. Do you know the nigga brought his girl with us at the last minute? I could've stayed home for all of that shit. Man, they were fighting the whole time! He even left her at a gas station off the highway for talking shit. Then when he went back to get her she was gone. He started to panic and called the police talking about she got kidnapped by some trucker and shit. They wouldn't file a missing persons report for him because it hadn't yet been 24 hours, so he went crazy. We drove up and down the highway all night long; I even think the nigga was crying!"

"Hell naw! What type of bullshit was ya'll on?" I asked cracking up laughing.

"Wait a minute! Let me finish!" Tyrone said laughing with me. "Then after about six hours, he decided to get a room at a hotel down the highway from the gas station and guess what; she was already at the hotel when we got there, so as soon as she seen what room we went in, she called acting like the police. Then she came knocking on the door five minutes later. The nigga lost his damn mind."

"You damn right you could've stayed home for that shit!" I said laughing uncontrollably.

"Then after that, it was all about her for the rest of the weekend," he finished.

"I see, but look I am at Jasmine's job, so I will call you back when I am on my way through there," I told him. My pager was beeping at the same time with code 000, which was O's code. "O is beeping me as we speak. I will holla back!"

I waited to call O back because Jasmine was getting in the car. She had me a steak and shake combo as always.

"Thank you Baby," I said immediately opening up the bag and stuffing a handful of fries in my mouth.

"Thank you for coming to pick me up," She said kissing me on the cheek.

"So, how was work?" I asked with a mouth full of food.

"Not bad. I only worked 4 hours so it was over pretty fast."

"You must enjoy yourself at work; maybe I need to start coming inside so I can see who you enjoy about it so much," I said with my guilty conscious.

"Nigga please! You can come in all you like, as long as you ain't smelling like a dead skunk."

"Oh Baby, you know I was just kidding. You know I trust you!"

"I'm the one who need to be asking you what you did last night. What you got a guilty conscious or something?" she snapped.

"Girl I was just playing. There is no need to get all worked up over nothing. I just missed you that is all," I said trying to change the subject.

"We need to talk anyway," Jasmine told me in a serious voice.

"What's up?"

"I had a dream last night about me getting pregnant."

"And?" I asked.

"What do you mean 'and', most of my dreams have a meaning, so what if I am pregnant? Do you think you ready to be a daddy?" she asked me.

"Girl it was just a dream, besides, I can't have kids anyway. I done came inside a couple of girls before and it never happened to them."

"You sound stupid as hell! What do you mean you can't have kids?" she asked me frustrated.

"Look girl, I said I don't think you are even pregnant; and if you are than we going to get an abortion anyway. I ain't ready for no kids," I argued.

"Fuck you!" Jasmine said as she got out of the car in front of her mother's house.

"Jasmine! Look, I am sorry; I didn't mean it like that. All I am saying is that we are both young and that I wouldn't want to mess up your life the way mines is already. You can still go to college. If you got pregnant you would be stuck with a child," I said trying to fix our problems before they even got started.

"Well thank you for making my mind up for me. And if you so damn worried about 'us' being ready, then you need to wear a condom the next time your horny ass think about running up inside of me," Jasmine said slamming the door to the house in my face and leaving me outside to feel her pain.

"What's up Terry?" Jasmine's mom yelled at me from the back yard. "You feel like smoking one with me?"

"Sure."

"How are you doing today?" I asked her as she handed me the papers and bag to do the rolling with. All of her years of smoking and she still can't roll up a decent joint.

"You know I am glad you asked. Could you help me carry that picnic table over there, I am trying to set the yard up for the barbecue. I am sure Jasmine told you about it already."

"No, actually she didn't. She is mad at me right now."
"Oh, well you know it is her time of the month and she can act a fool around this time. She will come to her senses, give her a minute," she explained to me.

"I guess that explains everything," I said while laughing and firing up our joint.

"Hey, boy!" Jasmine yelled from the back porch.

"Uh, Oh," her mother said laughing at us kids playing the game of love.

"What's up sweetie," I whispered to her as we made our way into the house.

"John is on the phone for you," she said handing me the phone and walking away without saying another word.

"Hey, I am making a run, but I left that for you behind the couch in the basement. I will call you in a couple of hours to see if it was straight," John said.

"That's cool."

"I also talked to the Mexican and he ready whenever we are," he said before hanging up.

My pager was going off again, but this time it was Suds house with 000-911 behind the number. So I called back from the house phone. I knew it was O, and that he was pissed off at me, but yet and still, I took my time to call back.

"What's up," I said realizing he had been waiting on me for over an hour.

"Shit, you tell me. I've been calling you all weekend, and Tyrone and I been over here for 30 minutes."

"My bad, I been handling some of my business," I said putting emphases on 'my'.

"Your business? I need to holla at you about my business. How much of that shit do you have left?" he asked me trying to show me he was still the boss. He was furious at me, but still knew that he needed to be cool; he was on my territory, and I had his money.

"None," I said to show him that I was capable of saying fuck him and his money if I wanted to, which meant I was in charge until I decided to pay him his money.

"I will be there in about 10 minutes, so cool your horses cowboy," I told him laughing to reassure that I was going to pay him.

"Well hurry up! Tyrone and I was about to ride up to the State Line. I want to ride in that clean muthafucka everybody's been talking about," O said to show me he knew what I have been up to, but also that he had enough respect for the game to congratulate a young nigga making power moves. I instantly gained a lot of love and respect for him for his understanding.

I parked in the ally behind Suds house so that nobody would see me pulling a big trash bag out of the trunk.

"There my baby goes," Suds said surprised to see me walking in through the back door. "I almost thought you forgot about me. What is up with the trash bag?"

"Nothing, here put this up in your room for me," I said after grabbing a huge chunk off of it revealing its contents.

"Tea, give me a joint," she demanded, knowing that I trusted her not to steal any without me knowing.

"Woman you know you can have a joint," I said as I gave her a nice piece of the chunk I had just broken off.

"Look, my sister and her daughter are going to ride up to Michigan City Outlet Malls with us, so I ain't going to need the car anymore. Besides, I heard through the grapevine that you were on the way up to the line; just bring me back a case of Budweiser."

"Sure."

"How much money can I have for Pooh?" she asked getting straight to the point.

"How much do you need?"

"I don't know, at least $300," she said slowly like it was too much.

"Please, what you going to get her for $300, how about $600; is that cool?" I asked knowing it was and that I was simply paying my dues to the game.

"Is it? I love you so much Tea," Suds said hugging and kissing me on the lips.

"I love you too," I said caught off guard.

"Tyrone and O are on the front porch smoking. They probably don't even know you're here yet."

"That's good. Make sure you put this weed up good," I said giving her the look like don't take no more out of it. Then I handed her the money and headed out on to the porch catching Tyrone by surprise.

"What's up family member?" Tyrone asked. He was looking good too, with his fresh Fubu outfit on with the all white Reebok Classics white as snow to match.

"Nothing much," I asked as we shook hands and hugged. "Where is O at?"

"He went up to EK Mini Mart to get some more blunts."

EK is the neighborhood hang out, and is conveniently behind Suds house. We grew up hanging out there, so we are loved by everybody from the owners, which has changed several times over the years, to the kids we give dollars too; the kids that used to be us.

I instantly began to explain as much to my partner in crime as I could about what has been going on over the weekend. I told him about Suds daughter Sherrie, who he also knew from around the way, sucking me up; and about how me and Money took her friends up to the Marriott the same night. I told him about the weed and the Mexican connection that I had gotten through Jasmine's people, and how I pretty much took over O's clientèle, As I was getting into that, we were interrupted by O coming on to the porch from the back yard which was the short cut to EK.

"Why you park in the back?" O asked me while shaking hands and showing love.

110

"Yeah, where is the Caddy?" Tyrone asked to help break the thin ice.

"Oh, I had to get something out of the trunk and didn't want anybody to see me," I explained knowing that I could afford to tell them the truth. "Why don't you all come inside for a minute?"

As soon as we all got inside, I got O's money and gave it to him. He never even counted it. Then I gave Tyrone the weed I had to roll up so we could try it on the way up to the Michigan State Line to get our liquor.

I let O drive on the way. He was the OG, and no matter what I still had mad love for him. He never asked me once about anything that happened over the weekend and I didn't offer any more information than necessary. My phone and pager were both going crazy though, so I did know that I needed to get away from O as soon as possible. I didn't want to be all up in O's face making his money. I eventually hinted that I needed to get back to my grind. I knew that was a good excuse since he always teased me about being too ambitious.

After we said our goodbyes, Tyrone and I went to work. I showed him so much money and dope that he couldn't believe I didn't rob somebody to come up so fast. Then I showed him the weed as I sold it off pound for pound until it was almost gone.

The weed was so bomb that I never had a chance to call John to tell him about it. I already had his money for it, so I figured when I called him it would be for handling business.

With Tyrone's help, I sold all of the weed and dope by that next Friday. I was hustling so hard all week that I let my birthday come and go without any celebration except for hanging with Tyrone his girl Karee and Jasmine. We just hung out, went to a Japanese Steak House where they cook in front you at the table, and got drunk.

It was Friday morning; Sherrie came home for a weekend pass. This time I was sleep in the bedroom when she came in.

At first I thought it was a dream, but as soon as I came to my senses, I realized that I wasn't dreaming at all. Sherrie was sitting on the edge of the bed looking like if given the right opportunity, she would kill me.

"What's up?" I asked feeling caught off guard.

"Don't FUCKIN play with me. Mya told me everything you nasty nigga!"

"Girl you tripping, don't come at me on no bullshit like that. You ain't my bitch, so I can do whatever the fuck I want to. You are the one that was fucking a nigga all up in here when I came home. So get the fuck out of my face with that child's play."

"Okay, you want to play with me you punk ass nigga. We going to see who the fuck is the boss bitch around here. Oh, and I told Mya's man about ya'll little episode, so watch your back you lame ass faggot," she snapped letting me know that I crossed over that line between love and hate.

I paid her no attention at all. As far as I was concerned, she was all talk, so I went back to sleep.

When I woke up to my pager blowing up, I noticed that my car keys were gone. I immediately jumped up to see where Sherrie was, but to my surprise, she was in the bathroom doing her hair.

"Momma told me to tell you she is in your car," Sherrie told me like we were cool and never had a falling out before.

"That's cool."

"You need to get up in here?" she asked me.

"Yeah, but you can stay and watch if you want, or even hold me while I piss," I joked trying to see where we stood.

"Uh, you nasty!" she said with a smirk on her face.

"Well, if you ain't going to help, than get out," I said.

"I thought you said I could watch."

On that note I pulled it out and released that early morning load. Sherrie didn't pay me any attention either. She just kept doing her hair.

I got the phone and returned all of my calls. They were all business, except for a new number I had never seen before. I decided to wait to call that one back.

Money paged me too, and wanted me to meet him over Reds house later on. I told him that I would page him when I was on my way.

Then after talking to Tyrone and telling him I would come to pick him up after I got dressed, I went back and laid down. I can't say I didn't want Sherrie to come in the room, but fell asleep again. Instead of Sherrie it was Suds who woke me up.

"Tea, you know you need to get your lazy ass up. Everybody and there momma is looking for you."

"What time is it?"

"Too late to be asleep, are you hungry?" she asked me.

"Yes please. What you cooking?"

"Get your lazy ass up and come see," she said leaving the room.

As I got dressed I could smell the food cooking and hear Sherrie cursing her mother out for cooking me something to eat instead of her. There was enough for us all so I guess she did get her point across.

Tyrone was outside in the front of his house when I got over there. I gave him the weed to roll up as soon as he got inside of the car with me.

"I thought you had to take this car back today?" Tyrone asked me referring to the Caddy.

114

"I do."

"Then, why you smoking in it?"

"Fuck them and this car," I said like I was on top of the world.

I told Tyrone about my day so far. He told me to be careful with Sherrie, because she could get me caught up with her feelings. I agreed.

## **<u>Chapter 17</u>**

We pulled up in front of Red house to see that they were just leaving.

"Where are ya'll on your way to?" I asked.

"Damn, it took you all day. I thought you were going to page me when you were on your way?" Money said as he got out of the car with Red and jumped in with us.

"My bad, I fell back to sleep. You know you get up too early for me," I joked to him.

"It's cool. Remember what we talked about at breakfast last weekend?" Money asked me while hitting the blunt that I just passed back to him.

"Yeah, about the business."

"Yeah, that," he agreed choking on the weed.

"What's up?"

"Red wants one of those bricks but he said that he wants me to come along with you if he needs to send his money up front," Money explained.

"That is unnecessary. I can go get it and bring it to his front door. When will he be ready?" I asked him while rotating the blunt to Tyrone, who instantly started choking too.

"I guess now. Page him and put in my code 005; he will come back home to meet us," Money said.

I did page him and put in my cell phone number with Money's code.

"Hey, Tiffany and oh girl been calling me all week long. She said Mya been paging and calling your phone, but you ain't answering her calls," Money told me.

"That must be who was paging me earlier. Sherrie told me Mya told her what we did anyway," I said sounding lame.

"So, who the fuck is Sherrie?" Tyrone jumped in snapping. "You need to be trying to hook your boy up with one of them flippers, they the ones who talking about something."

"Nigga please! The way you all up in your girl's panties, how do you expect to have time to be out flipping with us?" I asked causing everybody to laugh.

"Fuck you niggas! Ya'll just jealous," Tyrone said protecting his relationship.

"Jealous. I ain't trying to be locked down like that until I am old, gray, and married," Money said while still laughing.

"I know what you mean Tyrone. It's just that I can't have all of that drama around my money," I told them both showing my only concern in the matter.

"Man to tell you the truth, I think you should move up out of there anyway," Tyrone told me.

"And go where? I can't get no crib or even afford one anyway," I said offended.

"What? You the one taking care of that house anyway. Just think about it: you pay all of the bills; take care of all of groceries; and not to mention still pay her to stay there," Tyrone said. "That ain't home my nigga. That is a rest haven."

"You know what it is? This nigga done fell in love with Suds. He feel like he got a family over there. Shit, you might as well be fucking both Sherrie and Suds, if you ain't already," Money said laughing, but I didn't find his joke funny at all.

"Naw that ain't it! I was just thinking about, you know, maybe ya'll both right. But fuck ya'll both, I ain't trying to hear that shit right now. Maybe I will look into finding me a bachelor crib somewhere," I said realizing that I was holding on to Suds because of the way she helped me when I was down and out. If it wasn't for her I would probably be dead or locked up by now. Still, that soft shit is what gets niggas killed daily, and they were right.

Red pulled up and we all got out the car to shake hands. I called John and told him that I would meet him at his mother's house momentarily. Then I went back to Suds' house to get my money and drop Tyrone off to hold down the business while I was gone.

I really didn't have enough money to pay for the whole brick, so I used John's $6,500 to go with my money and had plenty left over to give him some of his money still on top of that.

Jasmine and I sat outside on the porch while John went to take care of business in the Caddy again. We haven't seen or talked to each other in a couple of days.

"So, you don't come over to see me anymore, huh fathead?" she asked me tickling my side.

"No, I do not. As a matter of fact, I was thinking about leaving you for your brother," I said jumping up running away from her attack.

"Bye," she said acting like she was going into the house.

"Girl, sit your ass down," I said almost out of breath. "Look, I was just talking to Tyrone and Money about getting my own little bachelor crib or apartment. What do you think?"

"I don't think a bachelor crib will do you any good, other than getting you killed by me, but an apartment sounds like a great idea. You know I

hate you living over Suds house," Jasmine
explained excited about my idea.

"I know. Well do me a favor and get a
newspaper and circle some cribs in it for me,
because if I do get one I want to put it in your name.
Is that cool with you?"

"Yeah, as long as I have a key to it too,"
Jasmine said seriously.

I knew she was dead serious so I just left it
alone. John pulled up and his uncle Chuck pulled in
right behind him in this clean sky blue 1978
glasshouse Chevy Impala with the music swangin'.
It had California plates on it and not a spec of rust
on the body anyway. It had some 100 spoke
Dayton's with the vogue socks to match.

"Damn, that muthafucka is clean as the
board of health," I said not realizing that I cursed.

"Thanks," Chuck said. "My guy sent it to
me from Cali to sell for him. John just took me to
pick it up a few minutes ago."

John immediately gave me the eye, and I
instantly knew what it meant.

"Let me holla at you for a minute?" John
asked me.

"What's up?"

"Well, my uncle paged me when I left and told me he was ready; so, I waited on him."

"So, is he ready to handle business now?" I asked impatiently.

"I don't know. He wants to talk to you, so I will let you two handle all of that, but I am sure he wouldn't stop me from taking care of business unless he was ready," John said like he hadn't ever done any business with his uncle before.

"Cool," I said nervously.

"Terry, you want to go for a ride in it?" Chuck asked me referring to the car.

"Sure!"

"Can I come too, Uncle Chuck?" Jasmine asked sounding like a big baby.

"Maybe later, but for now this is a man's thang," he said sticking his tongue out at her.

Jasmine got the hint and just agreed, then went inside of the house as we drove off blasting that Mack 10 CD 'Who Banging'. I was nervous because I couldn't hear a thing and had never been alone with any man in Jasmine's family before, especially not Chuck.

"You like this car, Terry?" Chuck asked me.

"Yeah, I love it," I said sounding like I already told you how much once.

"Do you want it?" he asked me catching me completely off guard.

"Man, I can't afford a car like this!"

"Sure you can, I only want $5,000 for it. Anybody else I would charge $8,000, but you family," he said passing me the joint of Cali dro he had lit up.

"Still, $5,000 is a lot of money. Besides I am about to get my own place," I said intimidated by the price.

"How old are you?" he asked me surprised to hear me talk about my own crib.

"17"

"Damn, I didn't get my first place until I was 22 years old. You are moving fast. I will tell you what, if you want this car, give me $2,000 and owe me the rest. You can give me $1,000 every flip until you pay it off," he offered me.

"Are you serious?"

"Yeah, I am dead serious," he said laughing at me.

"Bet, I will have to bring you the $2,000 back."

"That's cool, and I am going to front you whatever you cop from me too," he just threw in like I was only copping an ounce or something: we were talking keys.

"I am trying to cop a whole key," I brought to his attention.

"I know what you copping. That is why I brought you two," he said while smiling.

"How much are you going to charge me apiece for them?"

"I don't know, let's say $18,000 for now," he said like it was nothing.

"That is cool," I said as we pulled up in front of Jasmine's house.

I told him that I will come back later on with the rest of the money for the brick and car. We exchanged numbers and I left.
Everything went cool with Red, so when I finally got back to Suds to drop off the other brick; I had enough money for John, the car, and the fronted brick. On that one flip, I made $6,000 profit, and it only took me a couple of hours.
My pager went off with 380 for Tyrone's code. I immediately called him back.

"O was looking for you earlier, and wants you to call or come by," Tyrone said.

"Why didn't he page me then?" I asked.

"Shit, I don't know, but he wants us to come by his mother's house in a couple of hours; they're cooking on the grill for his mother's birthday."

"That's cool with me. Hey, I am going to come over there to pick you up. I need you to put something up for me and ride over Jasmine's house with me," I said more so than asking. "Is that cool?"

"What kind of question is that?" he asked me.

"I don't know what you got going on over there. You know how your girl puts you inside them panties and then you disappear off of the face of the earth," I joked. "Give me 20 minutes."

I was in front of Suds house when I hung up the phone with Tyrone, and Sherrie was outside on the porch. The look that she was giving me made me instantly put my guard up. So, instead of leaving the brick there, I made a quick visit over to my mother's house before picking Tyrone up.

My mother and Jim weren't at home, so I snuck up to my lil' sister's room to hide it in there.

"What are you doing?" my little sister asked me seeing me sneaking around her closet.

"Just hiding something. I'll come back later to pick it up. If mamma's here I might need you to bring it outside to me," I said caught off guard.

124

"What is it?"

"Nothing, but don't mess with it at all. Do you hear me?" I said firmly.

"Do you have some money?" She asked me while rolling her eyes. I gave her $50 and made my way up out of there quickly.

"Don't light that up yet," I told Tyrone referring to the blunt in his hand.

"What happened to all of that gangster shit you were talking earlier?" he asked me sarcastically.

"I am on my way to drop it off; that is why I needed you to ride with me."

"Then what are you going to drive?" he asked.

"I got a few tricks up my sleeve," I said smiling.

We pulled up to Jasmine's house and as soon as Tyrone seen my Chevy sitting in the drive way, all cleaned up, he went crazy.

"Man who's car is that?" he asked flabbergasted.

"Mines."

"Stop bullshitting," he said testing me.

"Seriously, I bought it from Jasmine's uncle. You like it?" I asked already knowing the answer.

"Hell yeah I like it! Is that what I am driving?" he asked in a destructive way.

"No, you are driving the Caddy, at least for now anyway."

I got out the car and went inside to take care of my business. Meanwhile, Tyrone checked out my new toy.

"What's up?" I asked Jasmine's mother as she let me inside the door.

"Jasmine is gone with her friend Ebony to the mall," she said to me.

"Oh, I know, I was looking for Chuck," I said like I had business in her house that didn't concern Jasmine.

"What you want with Chuck?" she asked in a protective way.

"I am just bringing him a lil' bit of my hydro weed," I lied to her knowing that it was a good enough excuse.

"Oh, well he in the basement playing that play station. Tell him I said to roll me up a joint," she said knowing that I was lying through my teeth.

"Okay."

"And Terry, you be careful you hear me?" she said looking at me like she knew more than I thought she did, and that she only asked me to be careful around her daughter with my lifestyle.

"I will," is all I could say while holding her glance showing my appreciation and respect for her and her demands.

As I walked down into the basement all I could smell was chronic weed. That only added to the conversation with Jasmine's mother. I felt bad for not telling her a different lie, but what the hell.

"Here you go," I said as I pulled out a big zip lock bag from my underwear full of money that not even Tyrone knew I had on me.

"What's all this?" he asked me.

"Oh, that's $26,500 for you, the car and if you could give $6,500 of it to John for me. He ain't here and I forgot to tell him I was on my way over," I explained.

"Damn, you ain't no joke is you lil' nigga?" he asked me as a compliment.

"If you say so."

"Well as you can see, I cleaned up your car for you and took off the Cali plates. John got you some paper plates for me, but you shouldn't do too much riding around in it until you get it registered.

"That's cool," I said anxious to ride out in my new and first real whip.

"Well, here you go, and call me if you need anything else for anybody else," Chuck said handing over the keys to me.

"You already know I will," I said with an immature smile on my face.

"Hey, you be careful with that car. A muthafucka will try to rob you for it," he smiled back at me and gave me a quarter ounce of his Cali chronic. I accepted as I walked outside.

Tyrone was on my cell phone with his girl in the driver seat of the Caddy like he belonged there. I paid him no attention as Chuck showed me how to work the car stereo. Before you knew it we were on our way to drop off the rental car at the airport Avis.

## **<u>Chapter 18</u>**

After dropping off the rental car, Tyrone and I stopped by O's mother's house to holla at him. He had a look of both love and hate on his face when he realized it was us in that big body Chevy banging up the block.

"Nice ride my guy," O told me without going too far.

Everybody else at the barbecue who knew me acted like it was a Lexus Coupe. I kept my composure and instead of me marveling about my car, I just brushed it off like I been had it put up somewhere.

We hung out for sometime with O, and ate everything they had twice. Tyrone was still stuffing himself and making a plate to take home to his mother, so O and I slipped outside to talk and sneak into the garage to smoke a blunt of my Cali Chronic.

"You know, you really shouldn't be riding in that loud ass car with this weed on you, right?" O asked me breaking the silence.

"Yeah, I know but I just picked them both up at the same time, so I guess I had no choice," I said choking my lungs out.

"Man this shit is crazy," O said referring to the weed. "Where did you get this shit? Can you go get me some?"

"I don't know off hand; let me check for you."

"Hey, I know what you been up to my nigga. Don't think that I'm knocking your hustle or nothing. At first I was a little pissed off, but I understand your situation. Plus, you could never stop my people from being loyal to me, shit, I would rather them fuck with you than somebody else if I don't have nothing. Still, you have to be careful, because if it wasn't me, somebody else would've tried to kill you for stepping on their toes. I got love for you and envy the hustle in you; just don't let it get you killed out here in these streets," O explained to me like a man. He was cool about the whole situation on the surface, but I could tell that he felt betrayed on the low low.

"You know that I wasn't trying to step on your toes. What happened is I ran out of shit like the first night, and just so happened to run into this sweet connect from Cali. I didn't do anything but keep business flowing; at least that was the plan. But all of a sudden my bankroll quadrupled overnight and next thing you know I am on my feet. I just want you to know that it wasn't nothing personal, and that your clientèle is your clientèle," I told him feeling awkward about the whole thing.

"Man, I got so much clientèle that the little bit of them that you've been serving don't even amount to one hard days work for me. All I want is for you to be careful, that is all. Now, I do want to know if you can hook me up with that fire connect you talking about. Shit, a nigga need to grab something as we speak," O asked me passing me the blunt.

"Yeah, I can do that for you, but he only fuck with a brick or better at a time," I said trying to keep the business going the way the Mexican started me; even though I was no longer fooling with him.

"A brick! I know you ain't got brick money lil' nigga. Just the other day you were only grabbing four and a half and that was with Tyrone's help," O said smiling at me mysteriously as he talked.

"Well like I said, I blew up faster than I could have ever imagined over the weekend. Thanks to you that is!" I said giving him all of the credit for my success.

"Yeah, I see. Well how much for a brick?"

"$23, 000," I said slowly showing my weakness.

"Damn! $23,000. He got to do better than that," O said. "Tell him I will give him $22,000."

"Well, if you give me until later on I will go holla at him. However, I already know he won't be ready to move on anything until tomorrow morning."

I knew I could've easily went to my mother's house and grabbed the brick that I left over there and sold it to him. As a matter of fact, I was sure I was going to give it to him for $22,000, because I didn't give Red a good price like that and I didn't want him or anybody else to know that it was my decision to make.

After I dropped Tyrone off at home to hook up with his girlfriend, I went back over Jasmine's house to pick her up. She had lied to her mother about going to the mall, when really she was out meeting people to look at an apartment for me. Her friend Ebony was older than her, so she faked like it was her who was looking for the apartment, but was just going to still use Jasmine's information on the lease. It was pretty simple to manipulate when you got the money in your hand. All they cared about was a money order or cash, and a signature.

"I found a really nice apartment for you, but it is out in Mishawaka," Jasmine told me referring to an all white neighborhood on the outskirts of the city. "And guess what else? It has a garage too."

"How much does it cost a month?" I asked not really concerned at all.

"You will not believe me if I told you. I'll tell you what, let's go out there now. The lady gave us the keys and told us we can have it if we like it; and just to bring her the money and sign the lease in the morning."

"Okay, and how much did you say it was a month?" I asked again.

"$500, but all utilities are included," she said trying to convince me that it was the one.

"What is that supposed to mean?" I asked not fully aware.

"It means that you don't have to pay any bills," she said to me like I was an idiot.

"Oh, I like it already. When can I move in?"

"As soon as we pay her. She is a sweet old white woman about 70 years old. I told her it was for my high school sweetheart and you could see her heart drop. She said we are more than welcome to have it if we liked it," Jasmine told me constantly saying 'we' out loud.

I loved it! All of the floors were wood. It had two bedrooms and two bathrooms. It already felt like home to me. I had to bless the house by making love to my so called high school sweetheart on the kitchen counter top.

"You did a very good job at finding US a place," I said to her through my hard breathing and sweat. I made sure to put emphasis on 'US'.

"Thank you. That must mean I get a key," she joked at me.

"Well, I guess so. Maybe I should be asking you if I can get a copy of my own keys," I joked back.

"Good, because I was going to steal a key anyway," she said.

"Now why would you have to do a thing like that?"

"Because, you might be crazy enough to bring some hoochie momma up in here."

"Never," I lied knowing that she still lived with her mother, and went to school everyday. Little did I know, it wasn't as big of a problem as I thought it was.

I dropped Jasmine back off after we went to Olive Garden to eat. I really wasn't hungry, but felt like treating my woman for being so good.

When I pulled up in front of Suds' house banging my stereo, I saw Sherrie and a bunch of people outside. I instantly knew something was wrong, so instead of me parking out front, I parked around back.

As soon as I walked up to the back of the house I knew what the problem was. The back door was kicked down. Nobody saw me park around back so I had a split second to reflect on what I was looking at.

Then I immediately came to my senses. I entered through the missing door and saw Tina Suds shaking her head and washing dishes.

"What happened?" I asked.

"Shit, you tell me what happened. I got my baby up in here and don't need them coming up in here like that looking for you," Suds said coldly.

My first reaction was to just walk out, but then it dawned on me that I had kept a safe in the room. I went into the bedroom and just as I expected, my safe was an empty spot on the floor. Suds was right on my heels the whole time. I started to remember the feeling of when my mother did the same thing before putting me out.

"They took everything Tea, even all of your clothes and shoes. At least they didn't take none of Pooh Pooh's new school clothes I just brought her," Suds said coldly like I deserved what I had coming. "Look Tea, I am sorry for yelling at you. You know I love you like my own son, but this is stressful. I have a big whole in the back door and you know."

"Don't you think it is funny that they didn't take any of Pooh Pooh's new stuff?" I asked.

"Shit, that is a good thing," Suds said not getting my drift.

All I could think about was all of the things I had did for the day, and the only thing that I could come up with was Sherrie.

"Sherrie," I accidentally said out loud.

"What did Sherrie have to do with this? I know you ain't accusing my daughter of doing this are you Tea?"

"No. No. Tell her to come here," I said calmly not trying to tell on her.

"What was in that safe Tea?" Suds asked me.

"Nothing but a couple thousand dollars and a couple ounces. Why?" I asked curiously.

"I just hate to see this happened to you Tea."

"I'll be alright," I said knowing that she didn't' want me living there anymore broke. The streets were just cutthroat like that.

"Sherrie?" Suds yelled loud enough to make me jump.

"What momma?" Sherrie answered coming in the house. As soon as she saw me standing there she stopped in her tracks to show her guilt.

"Sherrie, what do you know about what happened here?" Suds asked her seeing she was acting funny.

The first look I saw on Sherrie's face was more of I'm sorry than an innocent look. We sat there sharing words between each other with nothing more than eye contact.

"Yes, Momma," Sherrie asked Suds coming to her senses.

"Tea wanted you."

"What do you want?" She was saying like I better not blame her for what happened.

"I need you to ride somewhere with me," I said as if I might be planning on killing her and dumping her body somewhere she would never be found.

"Where?" she asked scared.

"Yeah, Tea, where do you need Sherrie to ride with you to?" Suds asked.

"Why all of a sudden do it feel like ya'll don't trust me anymore? All I asked is if she would ride somewhere with me. That place could be to the movies or anywhere else."

"Well then I am definitely coming too," Suds said trying to figure me out but couldn't. She didn't understand how I was acting so cool after just being robbed.

"No Momma. I will go with Tea alone, it's alright. That is if you don't mind," Sherrie said blushing and relieved. "Can I drive?"

"Drive? Hell no you can't drive. Tea, don't let that girl drive," Suds said glad to see everything was cool.

"Hell naw you can't drive," I said.

"Tea, watch your mouth, and I don't have a clue what you and Sherrie got going on, but I don't think I like it at all," Suds said jealously.

I had no intentions of taking Sherrie to the movies. I wanted to get her as drunk as possible; and if so, possibly get the truth out of her about what happened. I was positive that she knew who took my safe, and if she knew that, than she also knew they didn't find shit worth losing their lives over. That is exactly what it is going to cost whoever is responsible for what happened.

Sherrie was feeling like she was on top of the world riding around with me. We went all over the city, and she was in the passenger seat the whole time. After the first hour I had her so drunk and high that she knew she wasn't even in the car anymore than Tupac was as we blasted, 'Me against the world.'

I also knew that she would get in trouble for smoking weed when she went back to her facility; and, that she would lose all of her future visits and possibly not be able to get released on her scheduled date. This all of course was part of my plan to begin with; she must not have minded, because she is the one who insisted on smoking with me.

"Tea, I have to tell you something and please don't get mad at me for it, but, I love you and feel obligated to tell you what is up," Sherrie said slurring as she talked. She was sloppy drunk; her head was laid back on the seat rolling with the turns and pot holes in the streets that we drove over. "I know who broke into the house; I told them not to, but they told me to shut up!"

"You do?"

"Look, I am going back to girl school anyway for smoking this weed. You may think that I am too drunk to know what I am doing, but I am not," she said crying and then threw up all in my new car.

I was pissed off and for some reason feeling sorry for her; but, I needed to find out what she knew, so I just kept being patient.

"You think I am stupid don't you?" she asked yelling at me and looking a mess. "I know what you are doing to me, and maybe I deserve it, but please don't hate me Tea."

"I don't hate you girl," I lied. "I just want to know who took my safe."

"Antwan and Amp took it," she cried out while laying over into her own lap.

"I kind of figured Amp had something to do with it; but, who is Antwan?"

"Mya's boyfriend. After I told him about you fucking Mya he went off. He beat her up and then called Amp. Amp had already seen the safe in the room that day I had him in there. I'm so sorry! I just didn't want you to think that I set you up. Do you believe me?" Sherrie asked me crying uncontrollably.

I ignored her question because it was irrelevant. I was too busy thinking about getting my car detailed in the morning.

"Tea, look, I know I am not getting any more passes home, so I just want to ask you one favor."

"What?"

"Please fuck me before you drop me back off at home?" she asked looking a hot mess.

I guess after she threw up a few times she had sobered up a little. I looked at her and she looked miserable. Crying and just horrible, but for some reason I felt a little sorry for her.

Without saying a word to her, I went and got us a room at the Econo Lodge Motel on the strip. I had so many crazy things going through my head at once. I knew Mya had been trying to get in contact with me, but didn't know how much she knew about my safe. Was she also trying to set me up?

Sherrie really was a waste of time that night. She was so drunk that after she got out of the shower she fell straight to sleep. Then after a couple hours of me pacing back and forth from the window checking on my car she woke up.

She was laying there butt naked and a little sobered up, but still looking a mess. Her body was the only thing appealing about her. She was dark chocolate; with thick hips to support her huge ass. She had some pretty titties with some bright pink nipples that matched only the bright pink insides of her pussy. Sherrie was a freak though and very good at what she did.

After making me join her in the bed she stripped me down to my socks, and licked all over my body: my neck, chest, dick and balls, and even surprised the hell out of me when she started licking my ass hole. I hadn't ever experience any thing like that before and felt violated at first.

Then she climbed on top of me without letting me put a rubber on and rode me as hard as she could. From under her she was a beautiful site, titties bouncing with every one of our pumps.

"Oh yeah, apply pressure," she said holding me down tight wanting me to shove my whole dick inside of her without moving. Simply applying pressure: as much of it as I could. "Oh my god, I am cumming, please apply pressure."

"I am trying," I said getting all the way into her mood with her.

Next thing I knew I was nutting all up inside of her. In the back of my mind I was thinking about how she could get pregnant, but all I could do was enjoy the ride, for now anyway.

I only told Tyrone and my brother about Suds' house getting broken into and about me finding my own place. I hadn't been seeing my brother much over the last year because he was living the married lifestyle. He was living with this older babe who he had two kids by. After I told him about my little situation all of that changed.

## Chapter 19

After Jasmine and I got our apartment all straightened out, we went furniture shopping. I ended up putting the apartment in a fake name since there were no bills to pay or any credit checks. It all worked out perfect. If I would've known how cheap and easy it was to have my own place, I would've moved out of Suds house a long time ago.

I just put everything that had happened with my safe aside. For some reason I was afraid that if I told Jasmine about what happened, that she would unintentionally tell her family about it, and Lord knows that I didn't need my connect thinking that I was weak.

We went and got all of the things to make a comfortable but yet still bachelor setting. Then after we got everything we needed, I dropped her off to fix up the place so that I could go hook up and talk to my brother and Tyrone about what happened and what to do about Amp and Antwan.

I hadn't answered any of Mya's or O's pages yet, so first I called O and took care of business with him. He was happy about the price, and assured me that he would be hollering back soon. Then I immediately called Red who was also happy to hear that the price had changed and that I would be refunding him a stack. I knew that I didn't have to offer Red the difference in price that I charged him, but I didn't need the streets to be talking about my prices unless they were consistent.

Once I finally got over to Tyrone's house my brother was already there. He is a lunatic when it comes to his little brother, so he was already pumped up and ready to kill every bodies asses.

I told them about how Mya has been calling me and how I haven't answered any of her calls. They both were charged up and immediately encouraged me to not trust that bitch at all. I agreed!

"Look, call her and just play it cool; don't say anything about what happened. Maybe she will come off and give you a hint that she knows already. Then if she do, we can kill that bitch too," Romelo said while hitting the blunt at the same time. It was evident that neither of us had ever killed anybody before.

"I think you should ask her straight up if she heard anything," Tyrone insisted.

"I can't do that, because that will show my weakness," I said while calling her from my cell phone as we spoke.

"Look Tea, I heard what happened over Sherrie's house. I just want you to know that I had nothing to do with that shit. I was trying to call you before they even broke in, because I was going to tell you that they were planning on doing it. Why didn't you call me back?" Mya asked me talking too fast for comfort.

"Why are you telling me this now?"

"Because, you didn't call me back when I paged you," she said. "That nigga is gone have the nerve to hit me Tea. It is all Sherrie's fault; she plotted with them to set you up. She called them as soon as you and her momma were gone to come make it look like they broke in."

"She did?" I asked feeling sick to my stomach.

"Yeah, she told Antwan about us fucking; and, Antwan just mad because every since we fucked he ain't been able to get no pussy. Come pick me up and I will show you where Amp lives at."

"I will be over there in about an hour," I told her confused.

"Hurry up, because I miss you," she said. "Plus, I need to talk to you about something."

"What?" I asked curiously.

"Just come pick me up."

After I hung up the phone, I took a few seconds to recollect on what she said. I couldn't tell if she was sincere or not.

"I don't trust that bitch. I think the nigga was on another phone listening the whole time. Both that bitch and Sherrie set your dumb ass up," Romelo said frustrated.

"I agree with Romelo, but still, if we going to find out we should go over there. You drive in your Chevy and we will follow you in the creeper,"

Tyrone said referring to our little 1986 Chevy Celebrity with the dark tinted windows.

"If I see anything funny, I am going to kill everybody in the house," Romelo suggested again.

I was glad to have him with me, because I didn't feel capable of killing anyone. For some reason he was positive that he could.

Just as I pulled up in front of Mya's house, I saw Amp and Antwan both outside on the porch. I hadn't ever seen either of them before, but knew it was them because as soon as they saw my Chevy pull up, they pulled out there pistols like they were waiting on me to show up for the show down.

Before I could lower my window good enough, all I heard was rapid gun fire coming from the creeper that was pulling up behind my car. I saw both of them drop to the ground of the porch, but that wasn't low enough.

I stuck my same trusty 9 mm out of my driver window and shot the whole clip into their direction, not caring who or what got hit. Then I sped off with the music still blasting and headed straight out to my new place in Mishawaka.

Tyrone and Romelo stayed with me the whole way. We drove like nothing had ever happened. Police were flying with their sirens on into that direction. I was scared but still hyped up at the same time.

I parked my Chevy in the garage and was happy that nobody really knew the car yet. Besides, it was dark outside, so who cared.

We kicked it all night at my new place, drinking and smoking like nothing had just happened. Jasmine was enjoying herself just fine, she had a couple of her friends come by to show off the place and how well she did decorating it, so we made sure to play it cool.

I turned on my brand new 60" inch big screen television to the 11 o clock news to see if anything new had happened in the city, and just as I expected there it was. The story was on every channel.

"One dead and one wounded and in critical condition at the Memorial Hospital. There are no names being released at this time, but I can tell you that they were both young African-American men. There were several witnesses on the scene of the crime that say they saw an older car with loud music playing that was doing the shooting. More information will be available after the Special Crime Unit finishes with the initial investigation," the reporter explained causing my heart to just drop.

Jasmine was the only one of the girls who noticed that we were all looking guilty, but she left it alone. My first thought was that I was going to prison, but then I thought about the fact that nobody really knew I had that car. I was so confused!

"Good thing I put this place in a fake name," was all I could say when we were finally alone.

"Fuck that shit! If you go down, I go down," Romelo said meaning every word that came out of his mouth.

"Naw bro, I would never let that happen. You got too much to live for."

"Fuck that! If we have too, we will kill every damn witness in this city," Romelo yelled now drunk.

"It's cool," I said not actually believing the words that were coming out of my mouth.

"Well, what are you going to do then?" Tyrone asked me nervously.

"Nothing, I am going to act like nothing ever happened."

"Man look, I don't want you to drive that car anymore," Romelo said seriously to me.

"I won't. You know I ain't stupid."

"Well, I am going to work tomorrow, then I will come back over," Romelo told me to see if I would still be at home.

"Bet, but I will probably be over to Suds' house," I explained.

"What? That's the first place that they will come looking for you at," Romelo yelled at me.

"Exactly! I ain't running from nobody."

The next morning I got the paper and read the article. Amp was the one that died. He and

Antwan both had guns and drugs on them when they arrived at the hospital. I also got a page from Mya that morning, so I waited until I left the house to call her back.

"Was that you Tea?" Mya asked me with a shaky voice over the phone.

"No!"

"How do you know what I am talking about then?" she asked sounding like she was about to break down in tears.

"Because the shit is in the paper and all over the news," I lied.

"Yeah it is," she said calming down a little bit.

"Did you tell anybody that you think that I had anything to do with it?" I asked curiously of who the witnesses were.

"No, all I told the police is that they both stay into some shit, and that it was probably one of those Southeast Side Dawg Life gang members who was doing the shooting. Even though I think it was you."

"Why would you say some shit like that? I just told you that I didn't have anything to do with that shit."

"Look, I am not any snitch bitch anyway. If I did see you and I am not saying that I did, I wouldn't tell on you anyway.

"That's good to know, but like I said I didn't have anything to do with it, so I would appreciate it if you leave that situation alone," I said to change the tempo a bit. "So how is Antwan doing?"

"He only got shot in the leg, but that dumb ass nigga had all of that dope in his pocket and a gun on him when he got to the hospital. He better hope that the Fed's don't pick up his case. He locked up with a $10,000 bond," she explained like she was almost glad that he wasn't around.

"That is too bad!"

"Yeah, I guess it is, but like I said before; I don't fuck with him anymore. He was only over here to pick up his shit when he got shoot. Then all I heard was him out on the porch screaming like a little bitch. Amp ran almost a whole block before he died down the street on one of the neighborhood crack heads porch," she told the story to me knowing that I was interested in the fall of my arch enemies.

"I heard about that too," I said to encourage her to leave it alone.

"How?" she asked.

"The news!"

"Oh, yeah, that's right," she continued.

"Well, it was nice to hear from you again. I guess I will see you around?" I asked as more than a question.

"I sure hope so, maybe I will call you sometimes," she said inquiringly as well. "Or!"

"Or what?" I asked

"Or, we could hook up right now," she asked throwing me off guard. "I got my mother's car today, where are you at?"

"I'm on my way to the hood. Meet me over Suds house," I said not wanting to show that I am guilty. I knew better than to dodge her of all people.

"No, how about we meet at the Motel 6 on State Road 31," she suggested taking control. "I don't know if you remember, but I need to talk to you about something important."

"About what?"

"Just meet me and we can talk," she said finishing our conversation.

"I'll be there," I agreed.

Now I was very confused. I didn't know what to think about Mya. First I fucked her, then her boyfriend breaks in my spot, she tells me about it and said she would show me where they were at, and so conveniently, they are at her house when I get there. I shoot one of them and kill the other, and now she wants me to meet her at a motel room so that I can fuck her the very next day. She got that killer pussy for real!

## <u>Chapter 20</u>

I guess you could call me a sucker for love ass nigga, because not only did I go to meet Mya at the motel, but I didn't even tell anybody that I was going. She had already paid for the room, so she paged me and put her code 808 and 112 for the room number.

At first I thought about the fact that she was setting me up again, but then it crossed my mind that everything up to that moment could've been all coincidence.

As soon as I knocked on the room door it opened up and there she was, standing there alone stark naked. She was looking good as ever too, so I patted myself on the back for not listening to my conscience instead of my dick. And to think, I had my gun on me cocked and ready to shoot her or anyone else that was behind that door.

It only took me seconds to be undressed and up inside of her. She was a lot more passionate then before, and rubbed and kissed me all over like she had a point to prove. I would have to call what we did that day was made love to each other, because we were so gentle and caring that love was definitely in the air.

We started off just simply kissing and touching for over an hour. There were no words spoken out loud to one another, anything that we wanted, we had to earn from our actions. Body language was the only source of communication involved.

Then we moved on to making sure that we pleased our counterpart in ways unimaginable. I used my tongue to open up her legs so that I may explore her insides with my new found sex tool. I took my time to kiss on her outer layer of lips and thighs; then I licked over her hole like it was a lollipop at the state fair. Once I was sure that she was to the point of begging me for more, I took both of my hands and opened her secret hiding space up so that I could play hide and go seek with her clit. She couldn't believe that I was being so patient and waiting on her to cum before moving on to explore her insides with my magic stick.

I popped out her clit for the last time acting like it was a tease, but then I lightly took my tongue and ran circles around her clit for about 15 minutes keeping the same rhythm and tempo that I began with to show complete control over the situation. She came uncontrollably for minutes screaming out my name like it was on her mind, in her dreams, and most of all on top of her body: pleasing her.

I stayed at that room with her all day and night. My pager was off and my phone was off. We made love 10x's or more and was really enjoying ourselves. Then about midnight she messed up the entire mood when she told me what was on her mind.

"Tea," she said in her sweet seductive voice.

"What's up baby?" I asked sounding as young, dumb, and full of cum that I was.

"I haven't come on my period this month yet," she said changing from seductive to sad.

"That's a good thing isn't it?" I asked only concerned about being able to have sex without making a mess.

"Hell no it ain't a good thing!" she yelled changing the whole vibe. "I think that I am pregnant."

"You think you are what?" I asked finally getting the big picture, and not at all liking what I am seeing. "Why are you telling me instead of Antwan?"

"Fuck you!" she said slapping the piss up out of me. "Because if I am pregnant, most likely it is your baby!"

"How in the fuck do you figure that?" I asked holding my cheek and ready to punch this bitch in the face.

"You ain't ever wore no condom on me before. Shit, you just pumped enough gas in me today to fill up a semi truck. I ain't on no birth control that's how the fuck I figure that," she cried while getting dressed with tears rolling down the side of her face. "I am going to the doctor to see how far along I am, that will explain everything. Let me tell you now before you get any bright ideas. If it's yours I am keeping it, and if it's Antwan's I want an abortion and you paying for it or I'm telling the police that you killed Amp muthafucka!"

She was dressed and at the door now. "So, if I were you, I would be praying that the baby is

154

yours. And if I even hear about you denying mine, your life is over with bitch!" she said as she slammed the door leaving me naked, speechless and feeling stupid and fucked. I was so careless!

The truth was that she could very well be pregnant by me. I was thinking about that all the way out to my spot in Mishawaka. My pager was paging non-stop since I turned it back on. I had 187 pages from Tyrone and my brother at Suds house, so I made a detour over to there.

As soon as I pulled up and got out of my car at Suds house the police pulled up behind the creeper in their undercover Crown Victoria sedan. Everybody was outside watching them take me away. They found my gun in the creeper and held it up so that the Channel 16 news anchor could get a good picture of it. Then they asked me if I knew where it came from and whose it was? I sat there silent as a mouse.

They took me to the police station and again tried to question me, but again I said not one word. I didn't waive my rights to an attorney and I didn't ask for any of their cigarettes; I just sat there for several hours in the interrogation room silent.

They kept telling me that I was being charged with Murder and Attempted Murder, but the only thing that I was originally charged with was Possession of a Handgun without a License. They still had 72 hours to read me my warrant for Murder and with the holiday, that gave them an extra day to keep me in jail without bond.

I was booked into a cell house full of Southeast Side Dawgs, and right next to Antwan. He already knew who I was, but I didn't know him at first sight until he started making a trigger finger gesture at me like he was shooting at me. That tickled me, but I was not at all tickled about the fact that I was held behind enemy lines.

Being that we were in the same B cell house in the St. Joe county jail, we had visitation on the same day. He had been pulling his trigger at me through the cell house glass window and signaling off with my head signs for the last 24 hours, but once we were sent into that visitation room together, all of that stopped. I could tell that he was nervous, because his body was popping and shaking like he was in a dance contest.

His visitor was of course Mya. When she seen me her heart dropped out of her chest. Seeing her made me instantly recollect on the past night that we spent together, which was nice times. We both regained our composure and after she went down to Antwan, Jasmine walked up with a smile on her face that reassured me that I had a woman in my corner.

Jasmine was dressed to kill with a strapless top, tight fitting jeans, and had her nails and hair freshly done up. I could tell she was happy about something.

"Well look, John and Chuck both put up $5,000 apiece to retain you a lawyer, his name is Dre. Anyways he is black and supposed to be the best around. He said he will be down to see you today so be ready," she said nonchalantly. "And guess what?"

"What?" I asked not at all as excited as she was, or as she seemed anyway.

"Well, I got some good news and some bad news," Jasmine told me holding back to see my reaction.

"What is it girl?" I asked loosening up a bit.

"I'm pregnant," she said as if the lock was down on me, and I would never go anywhere.

"You're pregnant?" I asked thinking about the fact that Mya had just told me the same thing. "Are you going to have it?"

"I want to, but I am scared," she said releasing her true feelings through the tears running down her face. "I don't want to raise our child alone, that's what I..."

"You what?" I asked.

"Look, I ain't going to put no more pressure on you then you already have. Just worry about getting out first. Your lawyer said that if they do charge you that he might be able to get you a bond."

"He lied to you, because there isn't any bail for Murder charges," I told her.

Jasmine cried out her last tears and then she straightened up so we could enjoy the rest of our visits.

Once I got back to my cell, they read me my warrants for both Murder and Attempted Murder. I was feeling small, like the walls were closing in on me.

My lawyer came to see me every weekend. At first he was talking about plea bargains: one for 40 years; then one for 30 years. Then once he seen that I wasn't going out like that he ordered to have a Fast and Speedy Trial date set.

He sent me a copy of my Motion of Discovery, and to my surprise, the only witnesses were Antwan and a crack head that I knew from around the way. Mya wasn't a witness against me and that was a relief.

I got mail from everybody: Suds, Sherrie, my mother, and of course the Streets. Jasmine had moved into my apartment and had a phone set up for me to call her and make three way calls for everybody in the cell block with me. Even the Dawg Life Gangsters loved me because I was also making calls for them because I knew that it was only temporary.

After I had been locked up for almost 3 Months the letter came from Mya. I couldn't believe that she had written. Antwan had just mysteriously been released for some unknown reason, so I guess she felt it was safe to write.

The letter was kind of sweet too.

*"Dear Tea,*

*I want to let you know that I am so sorry for reacting the way that I did about being pregnant. However, I told Antwan about being pregnant and he got so excited that I couldn't tell him the truth even if I tried. It would kill him inside! The truth is that I am pregnant by you Tea. There is no way that it is Antwan's because I am only like three weeks,*

*and if I add it up correctly that was around the first
time we hooked up. I am not tripping over you
claiming the baby, not just yet anyway, but it will be
up to you if you wan to be a part of our baby's life.
ANYWAYS*

*That isn't what I am writing you about, not
completely anyway. I am in love with you Tea, but I
know you probably hate my guts. Still, I felt like I
owed you a favor, so I had to play like I wanted to
be with Antwan again. I didn't, but it did workout. I
was able to convince him into not taking the stand
against you. I even told him that if I was him I
would offer you a deal for some money: he loved
that part. He said that if you paid him $10,000 that
he would testify on your behalf that he didn't see
you at the scene of the crime. I want you to pay him
the money, freedom is well worth any price. You
are my child's father, and I want you free to make
the choice as to if you want to be a part of our
child's life.*

*Write me back and let me know what you
think about what he wants. I can act like I talked to
Money about it or whatever, but he does not know
that I am writing you. I will also try to come and
see you this week.*

*Love,*

*Mya*

*P.S. 219-555-1234 call anytime after 9pm"*

"What an evil bitch," I told my lawyer after
reading the letter to him during our visit. "What
should I do?"

"Well actually, since he is the only reliable witness we haven't yet had a deposition with, it could work. I'll tell you what, I will call her and set up a deposition to get a statement from him, and if he keeps his story simple, I could possibly get all of your charges dismissed at a suppression hearing. He is the only reliable evidence against you. However, I can't tell him what to say, so you need to get back at her also," my lawyer said confidently.

"What about the gun?" I asked.

"The gun came back negative as a match to the bullet that killed him, and this Antwan guy only had a flesh wound so they couldn't match it up either. We would probably beat the Murder case, but they could have still convict you for the lesser charge of Reckless Homicide and that would stick. However, it would take at least another year before we actually make it to trial, and Reckless Homicide still carries a 8 year sentence," he explained.

"Fuck all of that. I am sick and tired of this place. If he comes through I will pay him the money. Set up the little meeting or deposition and I will call my girl to get her ready to drop you off the money," I told him. "Meanwhile, I will write this Mya broad back."

*"Mya,*
*I really appreciate all you are doing for me. You did clown me at the room, but that's alright because I had a great time with you. I've actually been waiting to hear from you, and to tell you the truth, I thought that you just might have come to see*

*me that day I saw you in the visitation room. I was
jealous! Come to see me, I already told my girl so
the coast is clear. I am sure we can work something
out.*

*Love,*

*Tea*

## <u>Chapter 21</u>

"It's sure nice to see you again," Mya said to me over the telephone receiver at our first visit. "You look like you are losing weight or something."

"Really, I actually think I gained a few pounds," I assured her in a jokingly manner.

"Anyways, I got your letter yesterday; you're so sweet when you want to be. I wrote you back too, so you should be getting it soon," she told me.

"Yeah, that was nice of you," I was trying my hardest to show fake emotions that weren't there. "So, what is the deal with your man?"

"Ain't nothing up with my man. I am only fooling back with him to help your ass out."

I was thinking in my head that this psycho bitch must really think that I am crazy. This can't be the same girl I met in front of Suds' house.

"I did talk to your lawyer and as long as you give Antwan the money he will change up his story," she told me with a mischievous look in her eyes.

"What? Am I supposed to give him the money first?" I asked frustrated.

"Yeah, we ain't stupid enough to do it without getting paid first," she snapped trying to catch herself when she said 'we', but knew it was too late.

"Okay, I will give ya'll," putting a strong emphasis on the word 'yall' so that she could feel me. "I will give him half of the money upfront, but if he even thinks about!"

She seen the expression on my face and understood what I said without finishing my sentence. "Don't worry about that. He will do the right thing."

"Lets all hope so!" I said before hanging up the receiver and walking out of the visitation room.

Weeks had gone by since Mya had visited me. I hadn't heard anything from my lawyer and was starting to get frustrated. Jasmine was starting to show and quit school because she was embarrassed of her belly. Everything was going all wrong!

"I talked to your lawyer earlier today," Jasmine told me as soon as she sat down in the visitation room. "He said you should be getting released any day now."

"He said what?" I asked looking at her facial expression, and it didn't at all match the mood.

"You heard me! You are coming home soon!"

Soon couldn't come fast enough for me. I had spent almost the last half of the year locked up behind enemy lines. I had missed so much in the streets. The last time that I talked to Tyrone he was telling me how good he was doing. He had came up dramatically off of the empire I built up. Plus with me locked up, O took the opportunity to get his own revenge by recruiting my right had man. I guess the streets are like a revolving circle, because every time somebody steps to the side another person takes his place. The funniest thing about it is how the streets don't mourn or miss you when you are gone.

My brother had gotten caught with a pistol and drugs on him and was also in jail, but in another wing called the J pod. I immediately had Jasmine post his bond, but still he was already a convicted felon. This case meant that the only plea bargain he would get would include prison time. My lawyer Dre took his case for me, and considering all of the money he was charging me already, he only charged him a couple of grand. With his bond being $3,000 on top of the lawyer fees, it ended up costing me $5,000. I would've paid $10,000 for my brother to get out; all I was worried about was him going to prison.

It was a Monday morning when they called me to go to court. I knew they had to be mistaken, because my trial date wasn't set for another 3 months. Either they had the wrong person, or it could be a good thing.

Immediately after arriving at the court house all shackled up, I seen Jasmine, Mya, and Antwan sitting in the corridor in front of Court Room 2.

*The Son of the Streets...*
*Terrence leRoy Baker*

Both, Jasmine and Mya where showing and looking like they were exactly the same amount of Months along, and Antwan couldn't look me in the eyes.

My lawyer Dre came into the courtroom rather late as he always did to make a strong appearance. The prosecutor was looking cocky and confident up until my lawyer approached him with some papers and the motion to dismiss all charges against me.

"This is some bullshit!" the prosecutor yelled out in front of everyone present in the courtroom.

The whole room went silent, even the judge who was explaining the process and any rights that you give up when you take a plea bargain to another inmate stopped to stare. There were at least 10 other inmates other than myself on the bench, and maybe another 20 people there to support or witness against us in the courtroom; all of which were caught off guard by the prosecutor's show of aggression.

The Judge called all counsels to the bench, and called "Order in the Court" to calm everybody's nerves. The prosecutor tried to plea his argument to the Judge, but from his outburst the Judge heard none of it.

As expected my case was called first, and to my surprise the prosecutor was seated with nothing to say. The judge explained why I was there, called if there were any witnesses, and after no response he ordered all charges against me be dismissed with prejudice, except for my Possession of a Handgun. He gave me time served for that and told me that I had to do a year on probation. I quickly signed the papers and shook my lawyer's hand.

After I was reseated, my lawyer approached me and explained why he hadn't come to see me in so long. I didn't care about any of that, and reassured him that I trusted he was doing his job.

I looked over at Antwan again, and this time he nodded his head my way as a confirmation that he did his job and appreciated the bankroll he received for it. I did not nod back to him, but instead smiled at his girlfriend. She was the witch behind my success. As they made their way out of the courtroom, she turned around and put her hand up to her face in a gesture for me to call her. I thought not, but who knew what my future held.

Even though the judge had ordered my immediate release, St. Joe County let you go when they feel like it. I knew it would be another 8 hours at least before I left. I had just ordered a $50 commissary order, and since there was nobody in my cell block from my hood except for my bunky Marcus, I decided I was going to leave it all to him because we already established a business relationship. I told him that once he got out I would put him down with me again, but until then, to stay up and to be careful. I threw a huge slam or spread, as it's called on the West Coast, for the whole block.

I cooked 10 Ramen Noodles, 4 Summer Sausages, 2 cups of Jalapeño Cheese, 1 Pickle, 2 bags or chips, 1 bag of Refried Beans, 2 packs of Chili, and 1 Tuna to throw a twist in there. I topped it off with all the Kool-Aid you could drink. Eating like this when you are looked up is called doing it big. This was a $30 slam, and it was better than a

*The Son of the Streets...*
*Terrence leRoy Baker*

Ruth Chris steak; well maybe not as good as Ruth Chris, but it was good.

      After stuffing myself and telling everybody to kiss my ass, I went in my room and slept until they called my name at about midnight.

## Chapter 22

Back on the streets again. I remember dreaming about the day I would be free again and realizing that it could be a lot of years. Now I look at Jasmine as she picked me up, and feel lost in the world of freedom.

Nothing was the way that I had left it. Jasmine was big and pregnant, I was next to being broke, and only had one thing on my mind and that was getting money. My little bachelor crib had baby beds in it; plus, Jasmine had more clothes in my closet than me.

I didn't realize in all of the sexual dreams and fantasies that I had in jail that Jasmine would be so big and pregnant. However, the sex was still good, other than the fact that the whole time all I was thinking about was if I was really ready for a family. Funny how I could come to such a conclusion like that when my woman was almost due.

I swore to myself that no matter how I felt, I would always treat Jasmine with the utmost respect, she deserved it. I was going to be the best man and father to my child that I could be. I loved Jasmine because she let me be me and she was the only girl who was there for me when I had nobody else to turn to.

I waited for a week before I showed my face in the streets again. I needed to take care of family business and all of my debts that had accumulated over my incarceration period. At first I even considered getting a job and doing the right thing for my family, but all of those thoughts were erased once I made it with Jasmine to her mother's house.

"What is up jail bird?" John asked in a jokingly way smiling.

"Not too much, just trying to get back used to freedom. You could imagine how much I missed since I got locked up," I said while looking around me at everybody and everything that just looked different.

"Trust me, I can only imagine, and hope to never have to find out for myself. I might not get so lucky," he told me with an assuring nod.

"Lucky! I don't even believe in luck. I believe that people make there own luck happen for themselves," I said confidently, knowing that I had to pull a couple of strings to make my freedom happen.

"Well, I see you kept the Chevy all clean," he said while looking at my toy. "Are you going to keep it or sell it?"

"I don't know; everything has a price if you ask me," I said looking at my car and agreeing with the fact that it still looked good as ever. "It kind of has sentimental value now."

"Yeah, well be careful with my sister in it, because I would kill somebody for real if something happened to her," he said with a now serious look in his eyes.

"Trust and believe that I would've already killed who ever was foolish enough to think about trying me, giving them no chance to hurt her or my baby in her stomach."

"I feel that. If you need any help let me know. I know how that case knocked a whole in your pockets," John told me.

"Thank you. I will do that," I said while watching Chuck pulling up in the driveway in a brand new Thunderbird with some 18 inch rims on it. I could tell from his car that he hadn't missed me one bit.

"What's up Terry?" Chuck asked me. "Want to smoke one?"

"Sure, but let me warn you, I haven't smoked in months."

"Good, than that means you going to get blowed as hell because I got some Cali. Sometimes I stop smoking for a week or so, just to get that high you about to get."

"Oh, yeah," I said while getting into the car with him.

"So, how was your little jail bit?" Chuck asked me while passing the blunt.

"Not bad as far as being locked up, but man, so much has changed on the street," I said while holding the smoke in my mouth and talking at the same time. "Not to mention the fact that it was so expensive too."

"Tell me about it, we gave up $10,000 for a lawyer," he said reminding me that I owed him that money, but little did he know I came prepared.

"Yeah, I appreciate that; that's why I brought the money with me to pay you back," I said to correct his erroneous thinking.

"I figured you were good for it," he said caught off guard.

"That's cool," I said feeling high as a kite and looking at everything from a different point of view.

Jasmine was knocking on the car window telling me that her mother would like to talk to me. I told Chuck I would come back afterwards, but he was in a rush (so he said). He insisted on getting his money first so he could go handle his business, which from his body language I could tell didn't involve me at all. It didn't take me long to realize that he was cutting me off, which I couldn't blame him for. I was a young hot head ass nigga, so why jeopardize his business for my carelessness? I complied, and immediately regretted not just acting like I didn't have the money.

On the way inside of the house I ran into John.

"I think I might have changed my mind about selling my car," I told him with a heartbroken look on my face.

"You might as well get rid of it, because you can always get something better. Remember that in this game, it always gets greater later," John told me making me feel a little better. "I'll tell you what, throw me the keys and I will take it over to my Mexican buddies house so that he can look at it."

"Bet," I said tossing him the keys as I was entering the house.

Jasmine's mother makes the best Gumbo in the state. I was fortunate enough to already have a bowl ready for me when I got inside of the kitchen.

"Hey, Terry," she said smiling, but I could tell that she wasn't really happy to see me.

"How are you doing?" I asked feeling the heat from her vibe as I took a seat on the available bar stool.

"You know I never had a chance to talk to you about how disappointed I am in both you and Jasmine," she said while holding my gaze.

"I am sorry, I was careless."

"No, its not just your fault. Jasmine is just as responsible as you are. I even tried to talk her into an abortion, but she insisted on having this baby. You do not have a clue how much you've missed out on already. I only ask one thing of you both; I want my baby to finish school," she finished as she and I both noticed Jasmine crying from our conversation.

"I promise you she will. We already have been talking about night school, and I promise I will take good care of my child."

"That's another thing that I would like to talk to you about. I think it would be better for everyone if Jasmine moves back home. Actually when I put her out, I was under the impression that she had no where else to go and would hopefully come to her senses about getting an abortion. I was wrong," her mother said coldly.

"Oh, I never knew that was what she got put out about. Well I really appreciate your concern, but Jasmine and I are a family, and I don't think that it will be necessary for her to move out of our home," I said while I finished my bowl of gumbo. "And thanks for the gumbo, as always, it was delicious."

Right then and there my whole way of looking at Jasmine, myself, and my life all changed. Seeing Jasmine crying and standing up for me touched my heart so deeply that I too had tears in my eyes, but had to be strong for my woman.
    On the way out of the house I looked back at Jasmine and her mother, and noticed her mother was smiling and embracing her daughter with open arms. I seen life before my eyes and right at that moment I felt like a man for the first time in my

life. I was willing to fight and protect the one and only thing that mattered: my family.

I went and sat down on the front porch to relax and wait for John who was gone in my car still. Jasmine momentarily came out behind me and took a seat beside her man.

"Thank you. That was so sweet of you to say the things you said. My mother said she thinks I made a good choice and could tell that you will be a great father," Jasmine said still sniffling. "You have to excuse me I get all emotional from being pregnant."

"That's nice to hear her say," I said noticing my car coming down the street banging. However, John was not driving. He got out of the passenger seat with a smile on his face and a bag in his had. Jasmine and I just looked at each other.

"You sold the car?" Jasmine asked disappointed and happy at the same time. "I never got a chance to drive it!"

"Don't worry about that, I will get you a car to drive soon, but right now baby, we need the money."

I followed John into the basement and told Jasmine to sneak me another bowl of gumbo. I had the munchies and knew John didn't want her in the basement while we handled our business.

"Well he loved the car and said to get his title for him. He also said he would give you a half

174

of a brick for it," but ended up giving me the whole brick and said I owed him $9,000.

"You think you can handle it, because I am sure he was giving it to you anyway: just made me responsible for it."

"Can I handle it? Give me 24 hours and I will bring you back the $9,000. I already have about $4,000 at the crib, so when you drop us off you can get that then. I will only owe you another $5,000. I still got the hustle in me. You may be able to take the hustler from the streets, but you can't take the streets out of a true hustler," I said with confidence.

## **Chapter 23**

So there I was: young, ambitious, and family orientated. The next couple of years went great for me, but brought trouble to my family.

Jasmine and I had a son, which was named after his father. He was my life! All I ever wanted to do was spoil him rotten. Yeah, I was very young, and not quite ready to leave the everyday thrills that come with the dope game behind. But still, I made sure that I took care of home first and foremost.

We ended up moving into a house even further out in the suburbs, but I still always kept me a bachelor crib and another woman on the side, which Jasmine would know about, but respect my space. She was a good understanding woman!

Our relationship had change dramatically, but our son was the most important thing in the world to us both. The wonderful sex life that we once shared before was now more of a job between us, and even sometimes plain boring; other times our sex would bring us closer together than we ever could've imagined getting. We became friends more so than lovers, and grew up together sexually and mentally. We did love each other, but it seemed like the more we got to know ourselves, the further out of love we became. That love was never wasted, but transformed into a friendship and partnership that will last a lifetime.

The other woman in my life was this younger girl name Candice. She was young, beautiful, and still supposedly a virgin when I met her. Candice was tall, with long legs, and a red bone skin tone that made my mouth water whenever she was in sight. She had braces too, and silky hair that gave her a distinct look of a runway model.

I pursued Candice from the first time that I laid my eyes on her, which was while Jasmine was still pregnant. Candice lived on the North Side, so it was just convenient to be around her all of the time. She also smoked weed as well, and that would become the skeleton key to her heart and panties in the future.

However, it did take me a long time to trick her into believing that I was worth her goodies. I even had to give her oral pleasures several times before she actually gave into me; I never realized at the time how me giving her such good oral pleasure first, before sex, would turn her out into a crazy, possessive, love freak for me.

In Candice's eyes, she was my girlfriend, and she was willing to do and hurt anybody that stood in her way. She beat up any girl who looked at me, and even got out of line and fought my woman Jasmine and Sherrie within the first year of our relationship.

I was a sucker for love too. Candice had some of the sweetest, juiciest, and deepest pussy that I had ever had. From the first time I ate her pussy, I promised her that I would never leave her. I even told her that I loved her before that. After she finally felt that she had me all wrapped around her clit good enough, she gave it to me, and with all of the drama that came with it too.

While living at home with Jasmine, I kept Candice on the side for the first couple of years of our son's life. But, after I took Candice to our house while Jasmine was at work and Candice called her house to put our home number on her caller I D, Jasmine had had enough.

That day was so crazy. When I came home like nothing had happened and seen the look on Jasmine's face as Candice explained to her the color of our furniture and the way our house was arranged. All I could do was look like the stupid fool that I was for taking her home in the first place.

Jasmine put me out that night; then like the sucker for love that I was I ran straight to Candice's house to find out that she was gone with another man. I knew that I had messed up a great thing with a woman who loved me for me, for a woman who loved me for nothing more than sex and money.

Over the next couple of years, Jasmine and I grew apart. She started to really hate my guts. She would even mess with people just to get under my skin. I still would take good care of my son who became my best friend in the world. He was the spitting image of me, so Jasmine couldn't ever get the site of me out of her life even if she tried.

After Jasmine and I broke up, so to say, Candice stepped in big time. She had accomplished her main goal and finally had me all to herself, so she thought. I still had other women on the side, but she lived with me, drove all of my cars, and spent my money at will.

The craziest part about it is that after Jasmine left me alone, I took my hustle to a whole other level. There were no rules about coming home, or worrying about what was in the refrigerator to eat for dinner. I was free to run the streets, and had plenty of money to play with.

I bought a special edition 1980 Pontiac Trans Am: white with black plush interior, it had a

455 motor with t-tops, and some 20 inch 100 spoke wires and tires, just for sentimental purposes. I also had a 1995 Kawasaki 900r Ninja with chrome rims and a custom powder coat paint job. Last but not least, a practically brand new money green 1998 Cadillac Sedan Deville fully loaded, with some 20 inch flats, an in dash touch screen DVD deck and some 9 inch televisions in each headrest. I was the second person in the city with 20 inch rims; second to my good friend and playa partner: Travis O (RIP).

Now that I was free to run wildly in the streets, I would hustle all day and night. If I couldn't be there, I would send Candice, who became my partner in crime. She loved every minute of it too.

Actually, I was starting to feel like she was a good woman. We would drive down to Huston together so that I could cop from my new Mexican connect. Tyrone was in school down there at Lincoln Tech, so he made a lot of good friends who we ended up doing good business with.

Eventually, Candice and I too had fallen out. This girl named Jessica that I had known all of my life, who was claiming to be my cousin, got pregnant by me. Jessica was from Michigan; her auntie was my father's wife, so I basically grew up around her up until I stopped visiting my father's side of the family. It had been at least ten years since the last time I had seen her.

One day at one of my big barbecues in the hood, she showed up with another girl from the neighborhood. At first I didn't have any clue as to who Jessica was; up until she approached me and told me that she heard I was the one throwing the cookout and wanted to see me again.

Jessica was beautiful, and although she was black, all of her features were of a white girl. It was weird, because she had long blond hair, green eyes, and her skin tone was pale with freckles. There was something about her look that made me and every other man who crossed her path crave for her taste; something delicious that you never tasted before, and could only imagine how good it was.

Candice and I stayed together for the most part of Jessica's pregnancy, but Candice turned very bitter. I couldn't move around without her following me. She also started to steal money from me little by little, plus with the money that I would give her from helping me hustle, she had saved over $10,000.

Jessica, on the other hand, lived up in Michigan. So in order for me to see her, I had to travel, which I did almost every weekend. I really built strong feelings for her too. Maybe it was because of the drama that came with her being practically apart of my family; or the fact that it drove Candice so damn crazy. But I liked spending time away from everything and with Jessica. I even started getting money in the small town she lived in up in Michigan. It didn't take long for me to have a strong hold on that town too.

Money had become obsolete to me. On a good week alone, I would make over $100,000, so eventually my Texas connect, started to front me 10 keys on top of the 4 or 5 that I was already buying with my own money. I did business so much with him that he eventually started to have the dope dropped off to me for an extra $1,000 per key. He had a strong hold on the Chicago market, which was only an hour away from South Bend, so having the dope dropped off was only a shot call away for him all the way down in Texas.

I did have a lot of love for Candice; it seemed like over the years of our relationship that she grew even more beautiful. She no longer wore braces, and had blossomed dramatically all the way around.

All of the other dealers, both young and old, was trying to pursue Candice, and with me spending so much time in Michigan, she was an easy target. I would hear about how she was at different parties and clubs while I was gone out of town, and about how she was cheating on me behind my back.

One weekend I decide to stay at home. The first thing I did was try to make amends with Candice. I knew she loved me enough to forget all of my absences, so I romanced her trying to win her heart back.

"Baby, lets go down to Indianapolis and look for us an apartment down there," I asked her one morning after making love to her all night.

"For what?" she asked. "So you can run off and leave me every weekend?"

"No. I am tired of this same old shit around here; not to mention the fact that I am getting a funny feeling," I said while setting up on my elbow facing her.

"What do you mean a funny feeling?" she asked me curiously.

"I don't know; it's like I don't feel right or should I say safe around here anymore. These niggas been plotting on me for the longest, and not to mention the Fed's been knocking everybody left and right," I told her.

"Nigga, I know you ain't scared of these niggas all of a sudden, and the police ain't thinking about your lame ass," she said. "What you really worried about is all of these babies your nasty dick ass keeps making, and now your punk ass gone try to run. Just like a nigga!"

"You are unbelievable," I said laughing and lightly stroking her side while talking. Besides my brother and Tyrone, Candice was the only other person that I ever told about Mya's son being mines. She talked so bad to me for not stepping up and claiming him; however, she never told my secret to anyone. "Do you ever stop talking shit other than when I am fucking your brains out?"

"If that is what you call what you do to me, no I never stop talking shit! So if you're tired of my mouth then put something in it," she said while grabbing my dick and moving in closer to me for the attack.

We were already facing each other with only the rising sunlight illuminating the room. She came close enough for me to kiss her long and passionately without moving. Then I rolled her over onto her back and climbed on top of her body until I rested in-between her legs. Instead of entering her, I climbed up so I could spin my body around putting us into a 69 position with me on top. As I teased her, she started to lick on me. As soon as I went to work on her pussy that was already saturated with the smell of sex from the previous night, she took me into her mouth to let me fuck her face as deep as I wanted to without killing her.

Next thing I knew I was yelling how much I loved her and sweating up a storm while inside of her pounding away. Her long legs wrapped perfectly around my shoulders giving me perfect aim and access to her guts. She was enjoying herself; pulling me into her deeper and deeper each stroke.

All of a sudden out of nowhere I heard the front door get knocked off of the hinges. I was in the middle of my climax; so when I jump up and was about reach for my pistol, nut was still squirting out of me.

It was too late; there were pistols pointing at my head, both the big and little one. Speechlessly, I looked up at my masked attackers, wishing that they would've been the police instead of life threatening gangsters.

"Damn, that pussy looks good," one of them said in a familiar sounding voice. "Maybe I should get some of that pussy before we leave."

"Not yet," the one obviously in charge said. "But if this hoe ass nigga even act like he don't know why and what we are here for, than she won't be the only one getting fucked here today."

"Fuck ya'll! Ain't none of ya'll fucking me," Candice yelled while grabbing for some cover.

"Bitch, if you move again, we going to be fucking dead pussy," the familiar guy in charge said as he ripped the covers off of her.

Then he took off one of his gloves and grabbed her titty with such force that she screamed at the top of her lungs. He punched her in the face with all of his might. After that, he looked at me and then told his guy who was threatening to rape her to put on a rubber.

"Hold up," I interrupted their little party. "I'll give you all I have, just please leave her alone."

That was all I remember saying before everything blacked out. When I finally came back to, my head was bleeding and I was beat up badly, lying on the ground by the dresser. I looked up to find they were both taking turns fucking Candice in front of my face. She was screaming at the top of her lungs, and looking for me to help in anyway that I could.

When she seen that I was conscious down on the ground she felt a lot better. She knew what I was going to do, because I've explained to her why I had my shotgun strapped under our dresser. She started to fight back against their thrusts causing them to both have to take their minds off of me to focus on controlling her.

I reached up under the dresser to where I kept my 12 gage pump, and before I could turn around good I cocked it, wasting a shell because it was already loaded, but gaining attention. One of the attackers saw me and jumped to stop me, but he was too late. The first shot caught him in mid air coming at me blowing him clear across the room. As I cocked the pump again, the so called leader of the crew, jumped up out of Candice trying to reach for his gun. Candice kicked it out of the way just before he could grab it. He froze for a minute and just stared at her. I couldn't understand the look in his eyes, but it wasn't fear or hate; it was pain.

"Don't move muthafucka," I said to him as I stood over him sprawled on the ground. Tell your boys to stay the fuck out of the room or I will blow your head off.

"Tea, there isn't anyone else," he said to me causing me to finally recognize his voice. He then took off his mask.

"Money, what the fuck is up with you?" I asked not at all believing my eyes or heart.

"I am sorry Tea. She set you up and told me to do it. I never wanted to," Money said crying now and obviously scared.

Next thing I knew, Candice had his gun in her hand pulling the trigger, blowing his head halfway off with the information and reason with it. I was lost sitting there naked, beat up, and feeling betrayal all around me. Candice just looked at me with the gun still in her hands. For a minute, I didn't know if she would turn it on me or not. Maybe she was thinking the same thing about me; At that point in my life though, I really didn't care.

This was the first time I had ever witnessed anything as gruesome as rape, murder, and above all hate. It was in Money's eyes, Candice's eyes, and my heart. I never would've thought that my life would come to this from that one decision I made growing up. Everything was reflecting back to day one of it all: that first dollar I ever made hustling. My nigga Money who put me in the game! Now look where he is, dead; with me standing over his body, basically responsible for his life being over.

## Chapter 24

The police finally arrived moments later. Candice still had the pistol in her hand and I still had the gage in mine. We were both just staring at each other speechlessly. I couldn't even tell you how long we stood there, but all I knew was that I didn't trust her.

The police ended up taking both Candice and I into custody for Possession of Cocaine, Possession of illegal Firearms, Possession of Cocaine while in Possession of a deadly weapon; they charged us with everything in the book. I couldn't believe that they would treat us as bad as they did. We were the victims, but treated like criminals.

Once we got to the hospital, the investigators questioned us about every thing that happened. I refused to make a statement, but Candice gave the local police, FBI agents, ATF agents, Special Crime Unit, and every other agency full cooperation almost immediately.

Candice told them that I was a notorious drug dealer and that we were targeted because of my involvement with the streets. She even offered information about the Amp Murder case, and said that I bragged to her about paying off the witness in that case. She even offered to take the stand on me if all charges against her were dropped.

I was immediately taken to the St. Joe County Jail from the hospital. Lucky for me, I wasn't charged with Murder. However, I was still given a $100,000 cash bond, which knocked a huge chunk out of my pockets, taking me from sugar to shit within hours. Before I could get dressed into my orange jumpsuit good, my bond was posted. My lawyer was already contacted by Jasmine, who was the person there to pick me up when I limped out of the jail house, still dressed in my hospital gown.

"Are you alright?" Jasmine asked me with eyes full of tears.

"Not at all, but thanks for coming to get me."

"Everybody is calling me and it is all over the news too about what happened. They said that Candice got raped and that she is cooperating with the police against you," Jasmine said hysterically. "All I keep thinking about is how that could've been me and your son in that house with you."

"I doubt that seriously, because you would've never told on me," I said not wanting to mention the fact that the last words that came out of Money's mouth was that I was set up by my own woman.

"So, what are you going to do now?" Jasmine asked me in a concerned way.

"I don't know. After I go visit my lawyer tomorrow and find out what he thinks will happen, I will decide."

"Well I am going with you tomorrow then," Jasmine insisted.

"Why?" I asked not really wanting her sympathy.

"Because, I care about you. And if there is anything that I can do to help, I want to do it," she said starting to cry uncontrollably.

"Thank you," I said noticing that we were pulling up to her apartment. "Why are we here?"

"Please, boy, you ain't going nowhere but to sleep tonight. If you need some clothes, I will go get them for you in the morning," Jasmine said taking control of herself, and the situation.

"Well, then what am I going to wear until then?" I asked looking at my bloody clothes and sniffing my arm pit.

"Nothing," she said cracking a weak smile. "Besides, I still got some of your t-shirts and boxers that I stole from you."

"Is that so?" I asked glad to see that she still cherished my belongings.

"Yeah, but like I said before, you ain't wearing nothing," she said teasing me playfully as we entered the apartment.

After entering her apartment, I looked around feeling a sense of warmth and at home. Funny how tragedy makes a person open up their eyes and appreciate the little things in life that mean so much. At that moment I wished I could take it all back: the money, the cars, and the women. I wished life could just be simple again, but knew deep down that it never could be.

Jasmine looked different to me all of a sudden too. It was the first time I ever looked at her like a woman; she was always my girlfriend before in my eyes, now she stood there all woman. She had developed perfectly, her hair was flat-ironed silky straight, and her eyes radiated an inviting soft brown color that matched her smooth skin. I fell in love with her all over again, but knew that it was also too late for love as well. We could never be happy together again like when life was simple, because I crushed her heart into a cold piece of ice.

We slept together all night holding each other like never before. She cooked me a late dinner and I cooked her an early morning breakfast, but we didn't go any further than holding each other. It was almost like when we first got together; when I was homeless with nowhere to go, and I would sneak into her mother's house, where most of the time we would simply hold each other all night. All of the pain and struggles that life constantly dishes out was forgotten for that night. All of the doubt and insecurities of relationships didn't matter, because we were closer than lovers or friends: we were committed to each other for life through our son, and nothing or no one could change that fact.

I kept getting a vision that night about what happened. All that kept crossing my mind was the fact that I witnessed firsthand, my girlfriend raped, and the fact that I watched two men die. Yeah, I've killed before, but it was three of us shooting at the same time. I am not sure if it was my bullet or not that actually was the one that killed Amp. This time

I was positive of it; the thought alone crept me out. I felt bad because I had known one of them all of my life, he was the person who got me into this drug game. Now I was responsible for his death, whether I pulled the trigger or not.

The next morning I checked my voice mail, and to my surprise I had several messages from Candice crying and telling me how sorry she was. She said that she was just scared that she would end up going to prison. She also reminded me about the bricks that I had put up at her mother's house, which I clearly let slip my mind.

I ignored her messages and called Tyrone back, who had also left me several messages.

"What is up man you alright?" Tyrone asked me in a whisper like he was around somebody that he knew I wouldn't want to know I was on the phone.

"You know I stay cool."

"I heard what happened with your girl. The streets are talking! I knew that bitch wasn't good in the first place," he started lecturing me.

"You knew right," I said trying to change the subject.

"I heard she had been fucking that nigga behind your back anyway, I just didn't ever tell you because I knew how much that shit would've hurt you. Do you think they were fucking?" he asked suspiciously.

"Naw, I seriously doubt that," I lied knowing that if I told him what that nigga said that, he and my brother would both insist on me killing her or even doing it without my consent.

"Man, where are you at anyway? Everybody and they momma's is looking for you," Tyrone asked knowing I was lying and why.

"Jasmine's house."

"Oh, yeah!"

"Yeah," I said defensively.

"Well, tell the wife that I said what's up."

"She ain't the wife and you know it," I snapped in a respectful tone.

"She should've been; then we wouldn't have had all of these problems with you and all of your scandalous ass hoes," he corrected me. "You make a nigga think about settling down and getting married."

"Maybe you're right, but I don't need to hear all that bull shit right now. We about to go see my lawyer in a minute. I will call you back as soon as I leave, because I need a favor," I explained.

"We?" he asked playing with me.

"Yeah, you got a problem with that?" I asked.

"Naw, you cool. You may be a little confused, but you cool," he said teasing me.

"Look, I will get at you shortly. One!" I said as I hung up the phone not waiting to hear his next smart remark. He was my guy, but right now, I needed some space to think clearly.

## **Chapter 25**

"What's up my main man?" Dre, my lawyer asked. "A little beat up I see."

"Yeah, a little," I said while touching my face that was swollen up like a pumpkin.

"Have you talked to this Candice girl?" he asked me as if I would be plain stupid to.

"Not yet, but she has left several messages on my cell phone," I told him while looking over at Jasmine who was shaking her head vigorously. "She got some of my money put up and said she wants to meet up with me so she can give it to me."

"Well, if I was you, I would send somebody else to pick up anything from her, because she is now a Federal Witness against you," he said as emotionless as he could.

"What is that supposed to mean?"

"It means that your case has rolled over to the Federal Government. So if, and when you show up to court next week on your court date, they are going to drop your State charges and put you in custody under Federal charges. They will hold you without bond until your trial is over with or some type of deal or agreement is worked out. Either way, you are looking at a minimum of 10 years, and that is if you cut a deal."

"10 years for what?" I asked scared for my life.

"Well let's see, you got caught with over 1,000 grams of cocaine, 252 of which was crack; you had 6 guns in total, one of which was a fully automatic AR 15, all of which were loaded. That makes your case automatically Federal because of the fact that you had both guns and drugs in you possession at the same time. However, the crack is what is going to kill you the most, because the minimum on crack is 10 years alone with the feds," he was saying while reading my charges off to me. "Now I am saying 10 years because if you are willing to cooperate, then they will workout..."

"What? I ain't no snitch," I said cutting him off.

"Well in that case, make that at least 20 years, because if they wanted to they could charge you a year for every bullet and gun."

"That is ridiculous! Can't we get a better deal than that?"

"Look, this isn't like dealing with the State. The Feds go off of a sentencing guideline, and you score high on the point system. Then, there is the fact that you've beaten the State on a Murder charge, and are a known drug dealer. They will have no sympathy for you. Unless..."

"Don't even say it!" I interrupted him in mid sentence holding my hand up and keeping my head down. "Do you have any other good advice for me?"

"Well, you are pretty much screwed, so the only advice I have for you is to think about taking a vacation. The longer the better, if you get what I mean," he said sitting back in his chair and folding his hands across his knee.

"A vacation? How is that going to help me?" I asked not quite getting the drift. "Whenever I do come back I will still have to face them."

"Yeah, but if you are gone long enough; the case gets old; the evidence gets lost; the witnesses can't be found. Plus, if you don't show up to court, then you will have a State warrant for failure to appear, and the Fed's can't charge you until your case is thrown out of the State courtroom. That would be double jeopardy, so you will only have a Federal complaint against you as of now," he explained. "Now, that is where Candice could come into play at."

"What do you mean?" I asked him curiously.

"If she was to change her statement, it could make the Fed's think twice about your indictment. They hate to be made a fool of in the courtroom."

"She did mention that," I said quietly.

"I thought you didn't talk to her," Jasmine snapped jealously.

"She left me like 20 messages, it was one of them," I tried to explain.

"OK, look," Dre said trying to keep everybody focused. "You need to pay me $20,000 in full and up front on this case. I am only going to charge you as if it was a State case. I usually would charge more for Federal, but you've been a good client and seem to stay in trouble."

"Oh that is cold," I told him. "What's up with my brother's case?"

"He was going to have to do a few years on house arrest, but he didn't show up to court. So, they may try to take back their offer and make him serve his sentence in the joint."

"I will let him know what you said," I told him getting ready to leave.

"So, I guess I will see you around then. Be careful out there, and whenever you get tired of running, give me a call so I can get started on your case," Dre said standing up and giving me a strong handshake.

"Hopefully I will never have to call you," I told him. "I will have Jasmine bring you the money."

My mind was going 100 miles an hour. Here I was about to go on the run from the Feds. I couldn't tell anyone where I was going, and wouldn't know anybody once I got there. Jasmine was already crying. I was feeling her pain, but couldn't show it. I was scared!

After we left my lawyer's office, we stopped by Jasmine's mother's house to pick up my son. I wanted to spend the next few days with my son; and quiet as kept, his mother too. She cooked a big meal and for the first in a long time, we all sat down and ate together as a family. What was so crazy is how the last time, my son was in a high chair and I was feeding him. But now, he sat on his own and fed himself.

Jasmine's boyfriend, or whatever called and called, but Jasmine told him that I was visiting my son. He even popped up and got the door slammed in his face for showing up without calling first.

Over the next couple of days, Jasmine and I acted like a family together. We made love to each other every night, sometimes twice in one night. I was on a mission trying to get her pregnant. She didn't know what I was up to or, she did and wanted the same thing as me. Nevertheless, she never asked me to pull out or wear a condom.

"Where are you going to go?" Jasmine asked me late one night.

"I don't know. Why? You want to come with me?" I asked meaning every word that I said.

"I wish I could, but that is no way for us to raise our son," she explained sadly. "Plus, you and I are not the best of friends in the world either. You hurt me once; I can't let that happen again."

"Jasmine, I was young then. Now I am ready to be a family, besides, I can't tell that we aren't the best of friends," I said referring to the fact that we were definitely not acting like enemies.

"What do you think; you can just decide when you ready to be a family? I am seeing somebody else now, and he is good to me. I will help you out. I will even let you put a place in my name, but that is the best I can do. You don't have to worry, because I will bring your son to see you as long as it doesn't interfere with my work schedule. Tea, I am no longer in love with you anymore," she said in a serious cold voice. "I do love you though and always will."

"I need to use your car," I said jumping up out of the bed both heartbroken and mad.

"Go ahead, you bought it for me," she said with an attitude referring to the 2001 Mercury Sable that I had bought cash for her from the auction.

I pulled up to my house and saw that the lights were on inside. This was the first time going by or to my house since the incident had happened. After driving around back, I parked my car behind the garage and noticed that Candice's car was inside of it next to my Trans AM and motorcycle. My Cadillac wasn't there; I kept it put up in Candice's mother's garage.

The front door was fixed back up and the house was spotless. I came in through the back door catching Candice completely off guard.

"Oh my God, you scared the shit out of me!" she yelled at the top of her lungs. She was getting a beer out of the refrigerator.

I noticed that her face was still a little puffy, but she was healing up fine. Her eyes were bloodshot red though from crying for days. She was also thin like she hadn't eaten in days. I could tell that she didn't know what to expect from me and felt vulnerable and weak.

"You hungry?" I asked breaking the ice.

She immediately jumped into my arms and broke down into tears. "I love you Tea, I didn't know what to do. I am so sorry!"

I didn't say a word. I knew that she had been through a lot, and felt gross and used up. Really, I didn't blame her for telling on me. Most women would've done the same thing in her situation. Luckily, she still had all of her senses and didn't go crazy behind everything that happened. After being traumatized like that, she was actually being very strong.

We drove to Denny's in my Trans AM, she cried the entire way there and back. I told her that I forgave her and still loved her, which I can't lie, I did. That made her cry even more. I was feeling sorry for her, so I offered to take her on a trip out of town with me.

"Where to?" she asked sniffling in a concerned way.

"Trust me."

"I don't know if I can trust myself right now, but shit, I would go to hell and back to get you to love me again," she said sarcastically.

"I never stopped loving you," I reassured her.

After she took me to her mother's house to get my stuff, I promised that I would call her after I picked up Jasmine's car from our house and dropped it off to her. Then I would need her to come pick me up from Jasmine's house after Jasmine left to work. I gave her the keys to my Cadillac and told her to get it cleaned up after the "Touch and Shine" car wash opened up. It was still only 5 am. Excitedly, she agreed to everything, wanting to feel like I still was her man. I knew what I had to do, and what letting her drive my car would do to her.

Nobody had really seen my Cadillac around the hood. For some reason I feared that somebody would try to rob me. Guess it was too late for that! Another reason why I wanted Candice to be seen driving my new car, was because everybody was already talking about what happen to us, and how she told on me. I wanted the streets to see us as still standing strong and together. That way they would forget about the fact that anything was wrong with our relationship. People try to attack you when your guard is down, so I never wanted to show any signs of a weakness, or in this situation, a weak link.

Actually, I was talked about around the hood as a hero. My homeboy and his crew tried to rob me and I ended up killing them and getting away with it. I was praised by the youngsters and other dealers who had to worry about similar situations.

What people didn't know, not even Candice, was that I was about to go under and on the run to never return again.

"Where have you been all morning?" Jasmine asked me noticing that I had changed my clothes.

"Damn, you awfully concerned about my whereabouts to be in a relationship and happy with another man," I said playfully back to her.

"I ain't concerned, I was just worried about your punk ass. I thought that maybe that bitch you went running back to set you up for the kill this time," she said with an attitude like it was a serious joke or something.

"Look, I ain't got no time for that right now! I am putting something up in my son's room. Make sure that your nigga or whatever stay up out of there, because I don't need another Murder on my hands."

"That's supposed to be funny?" she asked me not at all feeling my vibe.

"No, but I am going out of town for a few days to find me a crib. I will be back to get my stuff after I find me a new city to take over," I said in a confident manner.

I gave her some money for my lawyer and some to put up in the bank for emergency purposes. She worked at a bank, so I knew that I would have access to my money from anywhere.

"Come here and let me smell your dick," Jasmine said stopping me from leaving out of the bedroom.

"What?!"

"Let me smell you dick, because I think you been fucking that bitch," Jasmine said serious as ever.

"You are crazy," I told her as I made my way to her bed side.

She was still laying in the bed and naked the same way I left her earlier. I just stood there next to her and let her unbuckle my pants and smell my draws.

"You can't get a good wift from the drawers; I think you need to get a little closer," I said playing along with her game.

"You think," she said as she released my growing hard member. "You smell just like pussy alright, but I think it might be mines. Let me taste it to see!"

I was horny as hell from her little game and that jealous side of her made me want her even more. She sat up on the side of the bed and gave me some of the best head I had ever had in my life; she took long, deep strokes of me into her mouth using her hands to guide and keep control while lightly jacking me off at the same time.

Right before I could nut, I pulled out of her mouth and then pushed her back onto the bed with force. Then I got down on my knees and put my face in-between her naked legs while putting her feet up on top of my shoulders. I had her wide open. My face was so far in her wet pussy, that I had a milky mustache when I finally came up for my first breath.

Without wiping the juices off of my face, I took off my clothes, and then I penetrated her warm sex haven. She pumped back invitingly with every one of my thrusts, trying to meet me halfway to our mutual destination of pleasure. As I pumped harder into her, she received me with more passion. Soon as I started to swell up and shake, she pushed me out of her, grabbing my sausage meat and ejaculating me off into her mouth, holding onto me and causing me to go weak and limp inside of her throat. She swallowed every drop, causing me to jump into the bed next to her and fall out cold.

## **Chapter 26**

Candice and I took a trip down to Indianapolis, IN. It was the Black Expo weekend, so the city was fat with parties and celebrities. I had a few playa partners who moved down to Indianapolis, so I made sure to call all of them.

We got us a room at the Sybris hotel; our room was magical. It had a Jacuzzi and a deluxe size swimming pool inside of our room. Candice was in awe when she looked around the inside of our suite.

The first night, we didn't do anything other than sip champagne and smoke on some good Naptown dowdy that I had my ex-bunky from the St. Joe county jail, Marcus, get for me. Marcus had also moved down to Naptown on the run for Murder over a year ago, so he understood my situation and was quick to help me out in anyway that he could.

Marcus was one year younger than me, but he still always looked up to me like I was his OG. I never understood why he had chosen to sell drugs. He was spoiled rotten, and had all of the finest of women, both young and older, loving him. Marcus was a high yellow pretty boy, who always dressed to kill in the finest of clothes. Other than the fact that he had gained a few extra pounds from stress, he was a true player in every since of the word.

He sold dope for me up until he messed up a few thousand dollars of my money. After beating him out of his brand new Nike Air Max's, I hadn't seen him around much, until I ran into him in the cell block in jail. We made amends and stuck together. We had no other choice, because we were both behind enemy lines. Then I promised to put him back down and never did once I got out. He was all grown up and more mature than I remembered him. He had his own hustling going good down here in the big city, so I had to give him his props.

When we all hooked up that first night, it wasn't him that tripped me out the most though. He was with an old dear friend of mine; he was with Charity. I didn't know if they were in a relationship or not, but what I did know is that I was struck with jealousy.

After we all met up at the local Red Lobster on 38th St., we got reacquainted with one another, had a few drinks, and told our own little stories about South Bend, IN. Come to find out Charity was in college at Purdue up in West Lafayette, IN, which was only 30 minutes away, so she would drive down to Naptown almost every weekend. She, like me, did the only logical thing to do when you go out of town, call up the people you know who lived there.

Charity and I spoke, but with Candice and Marcus both there, we left it at that. I wanted so badly to ask her what was up, and I could tell she wanted the same thing. Shit happens though, so I let that dream fade away with the goodbyes we all shared after leaving the restaurant.

Candice and I had a good time that first night together. We never mentioned anything about what happened. We just enjoyed our well deserved vacation with each other away from the world we lived in. I could tell that she had a lot on her mind though, because she would drift off and start crying for no reason whatsoever.

For some odd reason, I didn't want to have sex with her. I knew that she wanted too, but I just couldn't find her sexually attractive for some reason. She was beautiful, but all I kept picturing was her getting raped and hearing Money's last words over and over in my head.

"Tea, why haven't you touched me since we've been here?" she asked me looking at me through the heart shaped mirror over the top of our bed.

"What do you mean?" I asked giving her eye contact.

"You know what I mean. You never sleep with your boxers on for one, and for two, I am sitting her butt naked needing to be touch by my man and horny," she explained to me while pulling the covers back exposing her tampered with body.

"I didn't think that you would be in the mood for sex after..."

She grabbed me in her arms and hugged me close, tears falling down her face, and pulling at my boxers for me to get the hint and take them off. Usually I would be already turned on, but I was soft as a slug.
Still, she kept going: kissing me, licking on my nipples, which always gets the job done, but still nothing happened. I just laid there, soft as ever and not at all turned on by her.
"You want to know what is wrong with me? Well, all I can seem to think about is that nigga

saying that you set me up," I told her letting out all
of my frustrations.

"What? You believe that bullshit? I would
never do anything to harm you! Shit, you act like I
didn't just get raped because of your lame ass.
That's some fucked up shit to hear from the only
man that I ever really loved!" she screamed
hysterically. "Besides, I am the person that has been
telling you about Money all along. I knew he was
jealous of you, I could see it in his eyes!"

"Why would Money have to be jealous of
me?"

"Are you serious? Look at you and look at
Money. You run around here in your new cars,
dressed like you own the damn streets, while he still
hustling for Red. You can not be that stupid. You
even said all of this shit yourself. He is the one who
got you started, and you started acting like you
where too good for him and everybody else that
liked you when you were a nobody, homeless, and
flat broke on your ass. That is why he was jealous
of you, and now look, it cost him his life."

"You are talking to me about him like you
were feeling him or something. This nigga just
raped you remember! I wish I didn't have to see
him die like that; he was like a brother to me. I
knew his family and children. I am the Godfather to
his oldest son," I said to her with tears in my eyes.

"He was like a brother to you? Like you
give a fuck about a brother! You don't even treat

your own brother the way you should. Yeah, you may call your self looking out or whatever you call it, but nigga, I done sat up plenty of nights with you counting out more money than you even knew you had. How do you think that made me feel every time you wouldn't even know that you had 10 or 15 extra thousand dollars. I was even jealous of you and I was your so called girl. You don't trust anybody, and that is why Money said what he did, because he knew your fake ass would believe him," she cried out finally getting off a load that has been on top of her chest for possibly years.

"It is not my fault; the streets raised me this way. How am I supposed to be able to trust anybody, when everybody that I've ever trusted betrayed me, even my own mother turned her back on me. That is reality to me, and I know that my heart is cold. All I can do is be me. I can't live in these streets and expect to stay alive by putting my guard down for everybody who say or feel like they should have a reason to love me. I am scared of love, because it is so damn unpredictable," I told her with tears now falling.

"Tea, I am not saying that I agree with what Money did, but I too know what it feels like to be left in the cold by you. Here I've been the other woman in your life for all of these years; all of these years of hearing you lie to me about love; all of these years of watching you go home to your family, leaving me at home alone waiting on nothing to happen. I've still never been good enough for you though. You still have to go out and make a baby by your own cousin. Look at you! That is a perfect example. How could you do that to your family? Even if that girl isn't your blood, she is still apart of your family. You didn't care about nobody but yourself though, just like you always do; think of you first, then everybody else."

"So that is your excuse? You think that is a good enough reason to betray me? You knew what you were getting yourself into when you started messing with me in the first place. Now you going to act like you weren't selling dope and spending money right along with me," I went off.

"You think that this was about money? I do appreciate all that you've done for me, and like I said before, I do love you for real. Maybe I was wrong for trying to use that as an excuse, because I know I should've never told on you. I will change up my statement; even if that means that I end up going to prison," she explained with a serious face and sternly. "But don't you think for one minute that any of this was about money. This was about you and the way you treat people. You are running around your life with your head up your own ass, so it will not take long for somebody else to become your enemy."

"Why do you keep saying that you may go to prison?"

"I don't know, that is what they told me. But, as soon as we get back into town, I will do whatever I have to do to help you out. I will say that the police made me make a statement, which is not all a lie," she told me leaning back towards me for the first time since we started talking.

That was it; music to my ears and all that I wanted to hear come out of her mouth. I was glad to hear everything else she said to. Maybe I was a fucked up person, and to hear a person that loves me tell me that, made me want to change my ways. I just knew that wasn't an option at this point in the game.

She knew that whatever she had done or said changed the way that I looked at her too, because almost instantly, the satin sheets on the bed started to raise up in the dimly lit room. With her eyes blood shot red from crying and wide open from anticipation, she reached and took my growing pain into her hand. Smiling at me, she went searching for me with her eyes closed and mouth wide open full of hunger.

Within seconds she had found her weapon fully loaded and ready for war. She took me into her mouth immediately upon location, and gave me the most passionate head that she had ever given me before. This time there was stress, sorrow, love, and pain mixed into the equation, equaling a job well done.

Having had enough and on the verge of exploding all over her face, I brought her back up to the surface of our sea level of love. While making eye contact with her and still showing my hurt and disappointment without the slightest complaint and complete understanding, she straddled me slowly. Keeping eye contact with me, and with tears running down her face, she slid down on me accepting every inch of me while cherishing every second of our love making like it just might be the last.

She was enjoying herself too much, so I threw her off of me and stood over her mean mugging, an evil devious look. She was scared to death, then I forcefully threw her over onto her stomach and shoved my thumb into her ass hole at the same time as I entered her, making her scream and moan at the same time.

I forcefully pounded away at her: smacking her on her ass with my only free hand, yelling at her from the top of my lungs, telling her how she was a bad girl and deserved punishment. I kept pounding away until I felt satisfied that my point was across.

Even after, her ass cheeks were stinging and bloody red like her eyes. After she had a milky orgasm that ejaculated all over my balls and the sheets, I still continued my torture. I knew that she had never experienced anything so pleasing, yet demanding at the same time before in her life because it was also new to me and I was her first. I was reacting to my bottled up emotions, along with the harsh things that she told me about myself that hurt so badly because I knew that they were true.

This will become a ritual for me, and an asset to me for the rest of my living days; I will never have to worry about using my hands or any other physical force towards my women again. I learned that mixing pleasure with pain is the best and only way to instill fear and confusion into the hearts of women. I learned mental and physical abuse!

## **Chapter 27**


The next morning I left Candice at the room and hooked up with Marcus for breakfast at Bob Evans on 38th St. He was alone, which I was kind of hoping to see, but was also a little disappointed at the same time because I wanted to see Charity again too.

"So, where is your girl at?" Marcus asked me wondering why I was alone.

"She is at the room sleep. Where is your girl Charity at?" I asked him curiously.

"That isn't my girl, but she got mad at me last night, so I dropped her off at her friends house this morning."

"What did you do to that girl?" I asked knowing his reputation for dogging out women for no reason whatsoever.

"I didn't do anything to that girl. Shit, we fucked then I left her ass at my crib so that I could go out with my guys. She was trying to come with me and shit, like she was my women or something," he explained with a mouth full of food. "Shit, it is Expo weekend, ain't no telling which one of my hoes would have seen me out in traffic with her."

"Oh yeah, so you fucked her?" I asked jealously. "How was it?"

"Pussy is pussy!" he said cutting the conversation short.

"You can say that again," I said to him noticing something wasn't right in his eyes.

"So, what is up? I heard about what happened up in the Bend with you and your girl," Marcus asked me getting straight to the point.

"Well, I am about to go on the run," I told him.

"Why?"

"Man, you ain't going to believe me, but my case is about to turn over to the Feds."

"Why wouldn't I believe that? You been grinding up there for too long for them to let you slip through the cracks again like you did last time," he told me with a smile. "Shit, you know how long I've been on the run down here. They don't be tripping around here, I done got pulled over and everything several times without a license and they just let me drive off."

"How do you do that if you on the run?"

"I got the hook up on fake ID's. My dude from Atlanta can get you anything you want: credit cards, drives license, pass ports, whatever! Man this is the city; I got hook ups on cribs and everything. You should move down here, it is all kinds of money to be made around here."

"How much will an ID cost me?"

"$1,500"

"When can you get me one, I want one right now," I said reaching into my pocket to pull out the money and count it.

"Hold up," he told me while reaching across the table to me. "Let me call him first, to see if he is in town, and then I will call you later on so we can hook up."

"Bet, but even if you find out something, wait until I drop this snitch bitch off up in the Bend first. I don't want her to know what is going on."

"That is cool, but I still want to hook up with you so we can tear up the city in that Caddy of yours. You don't know how many groupies we can get in that muthafucka," he told me anxiously.

"Man, I ain't tripping on all of that shit right now, but we can kick it later on though. Just make sure that you check into that for me," I told him.

"I got you! Shit, I need one of my niggas down here with me anyway, because it is so much money around here to get that I be missing money. Then not to mention the fact that I been getting my dope from this Gary, IN nigga, and he is on some bullshit, charging an arm and a leg for some cut up shit."

"Well, you already know how I get down, so we going to get paid my nigga. Just don't say anything about any of this shit when we hook up, bet?"

"Bet."

Now that I had my biggest concern met, I could relax a little bit. What I needed more than anything else, was somewhere that I could move to and still hustle. Marcus already was in the streets, which was a good thing. But now I had a new problem on my hands; how was he going to take the fact that I will move down and possibly take over his business. Marcus was also on the run, so that meant that he was thirsty and dangerous. Once that desperation hits a mans appetite, there is no telling what limit they may go to for that next quick come up. These were all issues that I will just have to embrace for the time being, but as soon as I get my feet wet in my new city and soak up as much game from Marcus as I can, I will put some distance between his issues and my own.

After tying up all of my loose ends up in South Bend, I changed my phone number and left in the middle of the night without telling anybody that I was leaving. I gave Jasmine and Tyrone my number; my brother came with me. He had insisted on coming with me instead of showing up to court, so what the hell. I needed him with me actually, because it is scary moving away from your normal surroundings.

Marcus found me a ghetto ass crib on 34th St. and Moller in the Tara Apartments. At first I couldn't believe he would even consider me living there; but, once I noticed that it was directly across from a liquor store, Family Dollar, and Butler's Pizza joint, I quickly realized how fast I would gain some clientèle.

I moved all of my things down in a U Haul truck with a flat bed auto transporter on the back. This allowed me to put my motorcycle inside of the truck with my belongings, and then put my Trans AM on the auto transporter. My brother followed me in my Cadillac. As soon as I saw where I would be living, I immediately got me a storage unit from a local Public Storage Co. that I could use as my garage.

Shortly after arriving I was able to get my identification situation straightened out. But, before I could get my brother his, we ended up getting pulled over for speeding in my Trans AM, and he got locked up for his warrants up in South Bend.

My first year in Naptown was all partying, clubbing, and shopping. Every night Marcus had me up in a different club trying to take a new chick home. I bought all kinds of jewelry and clothes, and would eat out at expensive restaurants three times a day.

One day Marcus took me up to this car lot out east called Golden Rule. As soon as I pulled up in my Caddy, Fred, the sales man made me an offer on it. I knew that I needed to get rid of it, but never could've imagined that they would let me trade it in on a practically brand-new all black Cadillac Escalade EXT.

I quickly gave them my Caddy with another $20,000. They didn't ask me any questions about where the money came from or even my name for that matter. Even though I knew they were screwing me by telling me that I still owed them another $15,000 on top of all of that, I still couldn't resist the opportunity to drive away in that truck.

Then I went straight from them to my white boy, Mike Rudy, up at the new Mobile Jams on 46th and Shadeland Ave. He let me trade my Trans AM in for some 24 inch Dub Trumps spinners with the matching black background; an in dash Kenwood touch screen DVD deck with matching Kenwood touch screen TV's in both head rests; a pair of JL-10w7's and one JL 1000 watt amp to push them to the max; and, a custom Cadillac grill to go on the front of my truck. All of this for my Trans AM and another $7,500, I couldn't pass a deal up like that for the world.

Then, I rented a 3 bedroom house off of 56th and Georgetown Rd. with a 2 car garage, a fenced in backyard, and an outdoor Jacuzzi on the back deck. I put surveillance camera's around the house and a pool table in the living room. I finished up with a plasma screen high definition televisions in the master bedroom, on the wall above the fireplace in the living area that sat in front of the pool table, and one in the spare bedroom that I had turned into a pub, with a fully stocked bar.

About 3 or so months after I bought that truck I was practically broke. I was too busy trying to live that city lifestyle to maintain my hustle at the same time. All I was concerned about was buying more jewelry and clothes to keep up with the Jone's, so every time I would make a bankroll hustling, I would spend a bankroll at the mall. In the end it just didn't average out in my favor.

Then, one morning out of the blue, I got a phone call from Marcus' mother telling me that the police had finally caught up to him, and that he would be getting extradited back up to South Bend to face his Murder charges. I almost panicked, because my whole hustle had revolved around him; not to mention the fact that I had a $10,000 reward for my arrest.

I was paranoid, broke, and now all alone in this foreign city. It was time for me to get serious about my scratch. I was either going to sit around feeling sorry for myself while waiting to get caught up, or I was going to get my hustle on the way I knew how.

I no longer had anybody to go out clubbing with every night, so I knew that it was time for me to make a serious decision; I had to sell my truck. The one thought that kept crossing my mind was when Jasmine's brother John told me, "In this game, it always gets greater later." That was what I needed to have on my mind, thoughts like that. Who was I fooling anyway; I couldn't afford that lifestyle that I was living.

## **Chapter 28**

After I sold my truck back to Golden Rule, I was more focused than ever. They gave me a 1999 red Chevy Caviler to creep in, and $15,000. At first I was thinking to myself that I would be a fool to take such a loss on my truck, especially after I had just gave them my Cadillac and traded my Trans AM for the rims and shit. I gave them the truck back hooked up and worth more than it was when I bought it. However, Fred promised me that as soon as I was ready for another whip, that he would get me into what ever kind of car or truck that I wanted. That promise alone was worth taking a loss for, because I had plans for the future.

As soon as I left the car lot, I went to go hook up with another one of my friends named Socks, that had also moved down to Naptown from the Bend. Socks was a few years older than me; and he, like myself came up in the game messing with O. I was a youngster still when Socks was running the city. But, I still hung around him and O, so he knew me well and even witnessed me grow up in the game.

"What is up Socks?" I asked him as I entered into the barbershop that he owned and cut hair in.

"What is up Tea? Long time no see or hear, what you been up to?" he yelled as he put his clippers down to give me a handshake and hug.

"Man you know me; I'm just trying to keep my head above the water so that I don't drown out here."

"Yeah, I've been hearing about you being down here, but I haven't seen you around. I heard you was out here riding around in a big boy Escalade on some deuces," he said sarcastically in a way that showed me he was trying to say I need to cool down, but still giving me my props in front of his customers.

"You know how the streets exaggerate," I said blushing like a little boy. "But shit, I sold that truck back to the lot I got it from."

"Oh yeah, where did you cop it from?" he asked curiously.

"Golden Rule Auto."

"What? You fucking with them snakes up at Golden Rule? Man they the police!"

"Fuck'em," I said feeling like a fool.

"Why did you sell it anyway?"

"I don't know, I just felt like I was being too hot to be running from the feds," I whispered to him not trying to admit that I fell off because of the truck and could no longer afford it or the whole lifestyle that came with big truck driving.

"So what you pushing now," he asked me looking out of the front window expecting me to be in some sort of whip or toy.

"Oh, I am in my creeper; that red Caviler with the dark tinted windows on it."

"That is definitely a creeper," he said getting back to his customer.

"You got a long line?" I asked looking around the room at the 10 some odd customers.

"Yeah, but you had an appointment, so you next," he said winking his eye at me.

I sat down in a waiting chair and picked up a Vibe magazine off of the table. The shop was nice. It had a big screen television inside of the wall, with a play station 2 hooked up to it. There were pop and vending machines along the other wall. It also had a couple of female hairdressers that worked in the back. Some sexy females customers were walking out weaved up and pressed out, while chicken heads and hood rats were walking in to get transformed into something more than just a big butt to look at.

I guess I could see why so many guys came to the barbershop to just hang out. The women are much easier to holla at coming in than they were coming out. Not to mention the fact that the same broad would become unapproachable if you were to wait until they got all dressed up and out at a club. Of course all women don't fit into this category, but there are only a few exceptions to the rule.

While sitting there reading my magazine, I watched a whole society go on around me. Pretty single mothers came in to get their sons hair cut, bootleggers came and went trying to sell everything from jerseys, CD's, DVD's, to socks. There were even people coming in trying to sell soul food and pies off of a portable cart. The shop had it going on!

All of a sudden this fine honey came into the door with her son. She was a red bone with a dark short cut hair; hazel eyes that seemed yellow in the sunlight; and an intimidating presence that made every man in the room nervous. Socks, was finishing up on his current customer, so she walked right up to him like she owned the place.

"Hey Socks," she said to him while holding her hand over her cell phone receiver. "How many do you got in front of me?"

"One," Socks said hesitantly while giving me the 'my guy' look for approval of betrayal. "You must be in a rush ha, Trish?"

Noticing that he was looking at me for my approval, she looked over at me with those hazel eyes rolling in the back of her head. I couldn't face that woman so I looked back into my book trying not to let her over power me the way she would do anybody else foolish enough to stand off with her and her demanding eyes.

"Well, I guess they're going to have to wait, because I have an appointment," she said still facing me, and obviously not new to the appointment scam.

I laughed under me breath loud enough for her to hear me, but still looking into my magazine. Once I finally found the courage to look up, her son was already in Socks chair. Socks was looking back at me through the mirror on the wall with a smirk on his face.

Trish sat down right next to me, and resumed back to her conversation with her friend on the phone. There were plenty of other places for her to sit at, so when she chose to sit next to me, I got uncomfortable.

"Girl, these niggas done ran out of manners these days; a sister can't even get a door opened up for her or a chair pulled out at a restaurant. Here I am at the barbershop and I can't even get my own son's hair cut without fighting with a rude customer first."

"Excuse me," I interrupted her conversation knowing that she was referring to me. "Are you talking about me?"

She just smiled at me and then rolled her eyes into the back of her head again pissing me off and teasing me at the same time. "Girl I am up at Sock's shop on 38th and Lafayette Rd., and I think that it's one of his friends or whatever that was rude to me," she told whoever was on the phone. "You at the mall? Well come on up here, but I think I could take them both myself. Okay, I will see you in a minute."

"Look here Mrs. Thang, but I didn't say anything to you. Why you lie to your friend like that," I said feeling butterflies rise in my stomach.

"I know you did not just call me Mrs. Thang. Did you?"

"No!" I lied.

"I thought so. Don't act like you didn't say anything to me, because it isn't what you said, but how you looked at me that is going to get you messed up."

"You crazy," I said getting nervous, and not knowing if I should run or was she just playing a joke on me. I had no idea of what to expect. Trish was gorgeous, but for some reason, I pictured her friend being a big, bad, mean, bald headed sister with a serious attitude. She was the complete opposite.

"Hey girl," Trish said to her friend as she came into the door taking everybody's breath away.

"Hey girl! Now who do I have to beat up," she said looking around the room seeing several guys who would make perfect candidates. As her eyes fell upon mine she noticed the defensiveness. Trish just looked at me and rolled her eyes to confirm the fact that she had the right suspect.

"What is up Kelly?" Socks asked as he was putting the finishing touches on Trish's son's head.

"I'm cool, and you?" she asked while not taking her eyes off of me.

The whole shop kept staring at Kelly, she was a petite white girl with long blond hair pulled back into a pony tail. She had deep blue eyes that brought out the diamond necklace around her neck; and had an athletically built body that you couldn't help but notice from her legs.

"So, what is up with you talking crazy to my girl?" she asked me while sitting down next to me in the seat that Trish was sitting in.

"Please don't listen to anything that girl tells you about me," I said feeling back in control of myself.

"That girl has a name, and what is yours?" she asked me in her country-suburban mixed accent.

"Tea."

"Tea? That is not your name. What did your mamma name you?"

"What? You don't think my mother could've named me Tea?"

"Well then, what is your mother's number?" she asked me as she pulled her cell phone from her coach bag.

"Why?" I asked taking her phone out of her hand and dialing a number into it.

"Because I am going to ask her why she named you Tea," she explained as she put her phone up to her ear.

My cell phone started vibrating inside of my pocket, but I didn't reach to answer it. I knew she felt it too, because she was all up on me.

"What happened?" I asked.

"There was no answer, and your voicemail came on. You didn't give me your mother's number did you?

"Why you say that?"

"Because, why would you be on your mother's voice mail sounding all sexy and all?"

"Oh, so you thought I sounded sexy? Tell me this, how do you know I don't live at home with my mother, Kelly?" I asked putting an emphasis on her name, showing that I knew it.

"You just don't look like that type of guy," she said getting up to leave. "Well, it was nice to meet you, Mr. No Name."

"Nice meeting you too, Kelly," I said as I got up to take my seat in the barber chair. "Maybe I will hear from you again."

"Sorry, but I don't talk to strangers," she said keeping her position on my name.

"Hey Kelly," I said fingering for her to come close enough for me to whisper. "Terry."

"Well it was sure nice meeting you Terry, and I will hopefully talk to you soon," she whispered back into my ear sending chills through my body.

"I see you big pimpin'," Socks said putting the apron around my neck. "She likes you."

"Why do you say that?"

"Because, I've been cutting Trish's son's hair ever since he was a little baby, and Kelly usually comes with her up here. I've never seen her talk to anybody like that before. You know that they are both Indianapolis Colts cheerleaders right?"

"No, I didn't know that, but I do know that they are both fine as hell. What do you and Trish got going on?" I asked curiously.

"Well you know I cut a few of the Colts player's heads, so I usually get invited to they little parties. I was at Edge's party and she saw me lining his dreads up; asked me for a business card and been coming up to the shop ever since."

"I think she got a thing for you," I said raising my head up so he could cut under my throat.

"Please, all of them cheerleaders and girls that be at them parties be straight up groupies. I wouldn't take any of them seriously. They get drunk and next thing you know, they disappear one by one off into the bedrooms and bathrooms; that is if they aren't bold enough to just get naked at the door. You got a lot of that too; fucking and sucking on each other right in the front of everybody, both men and women," he explained. "They may all play that sadity role on the streets or at the club, but at them parties, they all groupie hoes, and they all end up too damn drunk to remember what happened the next morning, so they say."

"So that means that Kelly is a groupie too?"

"That means that they all are groupies, so if I was you, I wouldn't take her too seriously."

"Thanks for the heads up, but I wouldn't take her seriously anyway. I just met her," I said trying to stand my grounds against his groupie attacks.

"I'll tell you what, Cato is having a party tonight, do you want to go?"

"Hell yeah!"

"Watch, they will both be there, and I bet Kelly don't even speak to you."

"Shit, I might not speak to her! You put me in the room full of groupies and I will become an overnight celebrity. I will have every girl in that party thinking I just got drafted to the NFL on a 100 million dollar contract," I said looking into the mirror at my fresh haircut.

"You crazy! We're going to see how you act tonight. Just make sure that you dress the part. If you want a person to think that you got money, you want them to either see class or money when they look at you."

"Damn, I wish I would've never sold my truck," I told him sounding lame and foolish.

"Please, there will be so many trucks and Benz's out there that you could pick a car, claim it, and the groupies will believe you when you say it is yours. Just remember that you only get one chance to make a first impression, so make a good one. Then, it won't matter anymore what kind of car you drive, because once you associate yourself with the ball players and gain their favor, the groupies will always remember your face and flock to you no matter where you go. It's like magic!"

I sat there while socks gave me a crash course on "Groupie Love 101." Everything he said made so much since to me too. He told me that no matter who asked me my name at the party, to always give them my first and last name with a smile and handshake; this will make the average groupie think that I am somebody and that they should've known my name. That is groupies biggest thing, knowing the names and positions of all of the players on all of the teams. So, if they ever turn around and ask you your positions, act offended and excuse yourself from their presence. That will hook them and they will chase me around all night to apologize.

He also told me to be aware of the professional groupies, because they do know all of the ball players. They do research and study the sport just to avoid being tricked. They would get a kick out of exposing a fake, and also the ball players that have women troubles, they get a kick out of hating.

The best way to avoid these problems is to never tell a lie; never admit to anybody to be a ball player, it is best to let everybody assume it without telling them. What the eyes perceive the eyes believe!

## Chapter 29

After leaving the barbershop, I went straight up to Lafayette Square Mall to buy me a head to toe fit for the night. I had been out a thousand times in the Nappy city, but this would be the first time that I go out in the direct mix of the groupies and cheerleaders. They made every club in Nap the hottest spot in town to be at whenever they showed up.

At The Lark, I picked up an all black Azure linen outfit, some Kenneth Cole open toe sandals and a black Kango hat from Harold Pinor, just to set off the flavor that I was trying to create from scratch. My first impression was going to be one to remember, so I made sure to go to the extreme by getting a pedicure and manicure before I left the mall.

As I was finally walking out of the mall, I ran into a mutual friend of Marcus and myself named Stiff. Stiff was one of Marcus' go to guys in the streets, plus Stiff would usually go out with us to the clubs and parties, so I knew him very well.

Stiff and I always got along very well. Unlike Marcus, we were both silly and knew how to enjoy ourselves around women. Marcus would always play the pretty boy role, so he wouldn't say too much. I guess that worked for him, because he always would end up with the one girl out of the clique that didn't mind one night stands. I on the other hand, would always aim at the prettiest of the bunch. This usually meant that I had to play the dating game with them, which, always gave those long term results. Not too often do you run into a dime piece who wants to get flipped on the first night. Now Stiff would usually take the one that was left over, which 9 out of 10 times was the driver, so he had a harder job than us all. But if it wasn't for Stiff, the party would be over before it ever even started.

"What is up Stiff?" I yelled dropping my bags to give him some dap.

"Nigga, what is up with you? I have been looking for your ass for the longest. I saw your truck up at Golden Rule," Stiff said talking fast and not taking a pause for a breath.

"Man, I have been chilling. What you been up to?" I asked

"Just maintaining, its been hard on a pimp since my guy got locked up," Stiff said referring to Marcus.

"Tell me about it. I've been trying to find me a new connect myself. Ever since he got locked up, I haven't had anyway to get in contact with the Mexican we were hooking up with," I told him.

"What? I got the Mexican's number in my phone. Shit, I was about to call him myself, but I don't have any paper to cop with. I thought about calling him and robbing him for a brick or two," Stiff joked seriously.

"Fuck that, if you going hit a lick on a muthafucka, it better be for more than a brick or two," I told him also serious, but at the same time not knowing how he would react if he knew I was serious.

"Shit, why you playing with me, you know a nigga is thirsty?" Stiff said backing off of me a little to size me up.

"Yeah, you right. I will tell you what, I will call you tomorrow so that you can hook me up with the Mexican, and I will  put you on as soon as I get right," I told him.

"Or we could just say fuck him," Stiff said again pushing that issue to the limit.

"Who knows? We will just have to see what happens," I said now realizing how serious he was and how easy it would be to actually hit a lick. I had never thought about robbing anybody before. But for some reason, I was also feeling that thirst in my belly, and at that point where anything goes.

"What are you getting into tonight," he asked me looking at my shopping bags.

"Shit, I am going out to this groupie party or whatever my guy Socks got me going to."

"Where at?"

"I don't know why you want to go too?"

"No I am good, but just don't forget to call me tomorrow," Stiff reminded me.

"I got you my nigga!" I said giving him his dap on the way out of the mall.

As soon as I walked away from Stiff my phone started to vibrate. I had my hands full so I couldn't get to it fast enough, but once I got into my car I saw that it was Kelly calling me back already. Moments later my voice mail went off.

*"Hey Terrance, this is Kelly. I was just calling to say hello and to see what you are doing later on tonight. Maybe we could hook up or something. There is this scary movie that just came out by Wes Craven, and I wanted to go, but if you're too busy, I understand. Well call me back; you have my number. I am sorry I was mean to you earlier, so this will be my treat. Bye!"* Kelly said in her very sexy voice on my voice mail.

I was thinking to myself that maybe Socks was wrong about Kelly, but he did say she was digging me too. After I started my car and turned on the A/C, I decided to call her back.

"Hello," she answered on the first ring.

"Hey Kelly this is Tea. I mean Terry!"

"Hey. Did you get my message?"

"No," I lied to her wanting to hear her voice again begging me.

"Well, I left you a message. You should check your messages more often!"

"Yes ma'am!"

"I wanted to know if you would like to go out with me tonight."

"Man, you are moving pretty fast. I don't know if I am ready for a relationship just yet. I just met you today!" I joked.

"Boy you are so silly! I was talking about on a date to the movies!" she laughed.

"Oh, you had me scared for a minute. I would love to, but I kind of had plans tonight. Could we go out tomorrow instead?" I asked in a begging voice.

"Well I guess. Trish wanted to go out to this party anyway. I didn't feel like it, but oh well. Since I don't have anything else to do, I guess I will go," Kelly said referring to the party. She didn't know that I would also be there.

"I can't wait," I said sounding like a child who just got their way. "Why don't you call me later on to let me know that you made it home safe?"

"Maybe I will," she said in a naughty voice before hanging up on me.

## The Son of the Streets...
### Terrence leRoy Baker

I hung up my phone and sat back in the seat of my car. All that Sock said about the party and how Kelly would act once there was registering in my head. I knew that she would be there, but I didn't say anything to her about me being there. That will be a surprise. We will just have to see how everything plays out. I knew one thing for sure, and that's that I would be fresh to death.

## <u>Chapter 30</u>

"You want something to drink?" Socks asked me as I made my way into his bachelor pad. "If you do, look into the fridge."

I opened up the refrigerator and as expected in any bachelor crib, there was nothing but beer and hot dogs in there. I grabbed me an ice-cold MGD and turned the television to ESPN.

"Guess what?" I yelled back to Socks in his room.

"What?"

"Kelly called me and asked me to go out to the movies with her."

"She did?" he asked me while peeping his head around the corner of the hallway.

"Yeah, but I told her that I already had plans."

"Did you tell her that you were going to the party?" he asked me.

"Hell no, I told her that I had plans, not what my plans were."

"What did she say?"

"She said that she was going to go out with Trish," I told him while taking a big swig from my beer.

"I told you they would be at the party!" Socks yelled walking back into his room. "She just might speak to you after all!"

"She just might," I whispered under my breath to myself.

We made it to the party around midnight, so the party was already jumping when we got there. The party was held at Edge's house, which was a huge mansion that sat on the north side of Indianapolis in Zionsville. From the moment that we made it inside of the gated entry of his estate, I was amazed at the architecture. There was a wrap around driveway that surrounded a massive stone sculpture of cupid the love god. Once inside of the foyer, there sat a custom waterfall engraved in the wall that had a dim lighting from the crystal chandelier that hung from the ceiling down perfectly between the double spiral staircase that expanded three levels. All of his furniture was cherry oak wood with white leather: he had a cherry oak poker table, nightclub style bar, champion style pool table, dart board, and a custom cherry oak framed picture of "The Last Supper" on the wall over the fireplace.

The mansion was every bit of 25,000-30,000 square feet, giving all of the 200 or so guests in attendance space to move around and get lost if that is what they chose to do. In the back yard, where we were directed to, sat a full size swimming pool that was full of women swimming naked like nobody else was there. That sight caught me off guard though, because it was like nobody else but I even noticed them.

Socks was comfortable there like this was his normal hang out, while I was still trying to adjust to the fact that I was in the presence of so many millionaires. All of the Indianapolis Colts and Indiana Pacers were there, so my plan to portray a superstar was immediately forgotten. Between the fact that I was obviously out of place, and that there were so many beautiful women from all over the country everywhere, I knew that I would definitely enjoy myself.

Sock may have told me that all of the females at these parties were groupies, but what he failed to mention was how pretty they would all be. As far as I was concerned, all of the women there were wife material. We could get pass the fact that they were groupies fast.

"Terry? What are you doing here?" I heard a female's voice calling to me from behind me.

I looked back and there standing in front of me stood Charity and her college roommate Princess. The first thing that I did was looked them both up and down. Charity had on a black formfitting skit, with a pure white silk blouse that exposed her belly ring and made her curly hair stand out that fell down her back almost to her ass. She had on some white open toe stilettos that exposed her French manicured toes, and was wearing JLo perfume.

Charity was a natural beauty. She didn't have on any make up, and from what I saw so far, she was by far the most beautiful girl at the party. She carried herself that way too. I knew that my best bet was to let her be; either that, or set myself up for failure. Besides, last time I had seen her she was with Marcus and even though I always had a thing for her, I still didn't want to disrespect what they had.

Princess was wearing a one piece blue jean short Baby Phat outfit that looked dazzling on her extremely strapped body, grabbing her hips and chest in all of the right places to give special attention to the structure of a well proportioned sister. She had a short haircut that was freshly done up. Princess was looking delicious!

Princess was light skinned with dark brown eyes that yearned with the desire to have sex. As she looked me up and down I noticed her make a hungry sound as she came back up to meet my eyes with hers.

"What are you doing in here?" I asked Charity giving her a big warm hug. "And who is this beauty?"

"This is my girl Princess, she is my roommate," Charity told me stepping back so that Princess and I could shake hands. "I should be asking you what you are doing here."

"I am just chilling that is all. So, how is everything going for you? It's been over a year since the last time I seen you and Marcus," I asked her throwing his name out there.

"Please don't mention that name to me!" Charity snapped quickly. "That nigga ain't shit but a rapist!"

"What?"

"You heard me! That punk muthafucka better be glad I didn't have a pistol on me that night or he would be dead instead of locked up!" she told me with glossy eyes.

"He raped you?!"

"You might as well say so! He forced himself on me. Look at me, do I look like I can overpower his fat ass? I don't want to talk about it! I am just glad to see he is locked up and I hope they give him life!"

"So, would you ladies like for me to get you some drinks?" I asked changing up the conversation. I could tell Charity was getting emotional, and this wasn't the time or the place for all of that. Plus, Princess hadn't taken her eyes off of me since we ran into each other.

"Yeah, get me a white Russian," Charity said feeling like she had gotten her point across. "She will have the same thing."

"Hell naw, I don't want that nasty shit, get me some Moet," Princess spoke up for herself.

I ended up leaving them to go up to the bar. We were in the game room area of the house; there was music playing and some girls dancing. This area was like the VIP area of the house. All of the big money was in here, so as soon as I walked away from Charity and Princess, I knew that they would be preoccupied when or if I returned. That wouldn't really matter anyway, because I still wanted to play the field and see what else I could find among the masses.

As I was walking through the packed crowd of mostly women, I saw Socks trying to get my attention, so I struggled to make my way over to where he was. He was chilling with all of the players. They treated him like he was one of theirs.

"Where did you disappear to?" I asked him feeling abandoned and lost.

"Oh, I saw you talking to those nice honeys, so I gave you your space. What is up with them anyway?" Socks asked me.

"Them? I knew one of them already from the crib. They sent me to go get them some drinks."

"What is up young blood?" Edge asked me in his Southern Florida accent.

"I am good!" I said flabbergasted.

"My bad! Edge this is Tea, Tea this is Edge. This is his crib!"

"Nice crib!" I said trying not to scream from his firm handshake.

"Thanks! Tell your friends to come on over here and I will have somebody get their drinks," Edge told me in a welcoming, devious voice.

"Cool," I said already making my way back through the shoulder to shoulder crowd.

Approaching Charity and Princess, I noticed that they were still sitting where I had left them fighting off all of the males fighting for their attention.

"Where are our drinks at?" Charity asked me in a demanding voice.

"We moving over there," I told them pointing over to the ball players who were waving when they noticed them looking their way. I was getting a bad feeling about moving over there, but had nothing to lose. There were still plenty of fish in the sea.

We finally made our way over through the crowd to the table, and to my surprise the players were respectful to Charity and Princess. They treated them like they were my sisters and me like I was a close friend of theirs. I knew that they were simply feeling us all out, so I played along.

As I sat back between both Charity and Princess sipping on my Hennessy, I noticed that Trish and Kelly were looking at Socks and I. Socks noticed too, because he reached over Charity and tapped me on the leg pointing into their direction. I just waved at Kelly in a flirtatious way. She gave me an ugly look, and then motioned for me to come talk to her. I brushed her off!

As the night whined down, I had talked so good into Princess' ear that she was ready to do any and everything that I wanted to do; but, then out of nowhere, Charity laid her head on my shoulder. Caught off guard, I kept on chilling; acting like it was nothing. But in that split second, my whole life changed. Even though I was still facing Princess, I was no longer paying her the least bit of attention. I felt privileged to have such a beautiful girl leaning on my shoulder in the middle of a house full of professional ball players. Why me? Was she just comfortable with me? Is she too looking at me like a brother? Does she have any clue how much I would love to be with her?

I knew that the best thing for me to do was size the situation up and play the field: So many times before have I messed up for sure pussy like Princess, trying to get some more pussy. Switching up my attack now would show my weakness, and that would be too disrespectful to the game to be able to bounce back if Charity was simply just resting her head on a friendly shoulder.

After about 3 in the morning the party had gotten down to the few groupies that were staying for the after hours orgy session, so I knew it was time for me to make my move. Socks was feeling the same way, but he knew that we could both stay and join in the festivities.

"So what are ya'll about to get into?" I asked Princess loud enough for Charity to hear me too. Some of the girls at the party were stripping in the middle of the floor, so I was staring at the show and talking at the same time. "I am about to go down to the IHOP for something to eat."

"We coming with you," Charity said getting up as she spoke.

Socks wasn't at all feeling my choice to go out to eat instead of staying for some groupie love, but he still rolled with the punches. Princess still acted as if I was all hers up until Charity sat next to me in the booth at the International House of Pancakes, leaving her to set next to Socks across from us. I noticed the jealousy in Princess' eyes, but at that point of the night, Charity was already the only person in the restaurant besides me.

Under the table, we had our own little thing going on. Charity had slid her shoes off and laid her legs over mine to seal the deal between us; and, causing me to get aroused. Charity could feel me bulge through me pants; she just smiled. All of a sudden my phone started to vibrate, so Charity had to move her legs so that I could answer it.

Fidgeting, I reached into my pocket; seeing on my caller ID that it was Kelly calling me at 4 in the morning.

"Hello," I asked her rudely into my phone trying to intentionally stir jealously into a confusing situation.

"Hi! What is up with you?"

"I am good; glad to see that you didn't get yourself into trouble," I nonchalantly told her.

"Too bad I can't say the same thing about you," Kelly told me with animosity in her voice. "Don't act like I didn't see you at the party!"

Charity had obviously heard Kelly on the phone, because before I could reply she pinched me hard enough to draw blood. I looked at her like she was crazy, but as soon as I saw that fire in her eyes, I quickly backed down with a smile.

"Can I call you back?"

"Oh, you busy?" Kelly asked me without answering my question. "Are we still on for tomorrow?"

Charity pinched me again and then kicked her legs off of my lap causing the whole table to shake. I had no idea that this innocent beautiful woman could be so feisty. I hung up the phone on Kelly and just looked at Charity like the psycho she could potentially become.

After we ate and got ready to go our separate ways, I told them both that I had a great time with them and would keep contact. Really, I was trying to rush off so that I could call Kelly back. I had already messed up my all night event with Princess. Besides the fact that I didn't even know how to approach Charity with a night cap, losing Kelly too in the mix would mean disaster.

"Go ahead and run so you can call that bitch back," Charity abruptly said to me out of the blue. "I am coming with you!"

"I don't think that Princess wants to come over my house; not with you there anyway," I said joking.

"You let me worry about her," Charity said while putting her arms around my neck. We were out in the parking lot of the restaurant and the sun was starting to rise on the horizon.

Princess blew the horn on the car they were driving to tell Charity to hurry up. Charity walked around to the passenger side of the car and after a few seconds, Princess smashed off almost backing up into me on purpose, then burning a little rubber on her way out of the parking lot. Socks was coming out of the restaurant from paying the tab at the same time that she was leaving.

"What is wrong with her?" he asked both Charity and I.

"She will be alright!" Charity joked. "I don't think she thought you was digging her."

"Is that right?" Socks said while shaking his head at me in a disgusted way.

Finally at my house, everything was quiet and a mess. I wasn't expecting any company, so I had an excuse, but was still a little embarrassed. Charity paid no attention to my mess, and instead made herself at home.

She went straight into my bedroom and got partially undressed. She took off her skirt first revealing her booty cut panties; then she took her blouse off exposing her matching bra. I just stood there lost and speechless. At that point I really didn't know what to expect to happen. All I could think about was that I was about to have sex with the girl of my dreams.

After she made up my bed with a brand new "bed in the bag" that I was saving for a rainy day, kind of like the day I was having, she took off her bra and freed her perfect breasts. They weren't too big, but yet not too small; they curved up into the shape of a banana with big round circles around her perfect erect raisin nipples. They were perfect!

Charity had a perfect body, and with her hair falling down over her shoulders and down her back, all I could think about was her panties coming off next; but, never did. Instead she jumped into the bed leaving me fully dressed and to decide on my own what to do next. I felt abandoned inside of my own bedroom!

"Blaze up," she ordered me trying to intentionally take my mind off of her naked body.

"I didn't know that you smoked weed."

"What? Who don't smoke weed? Don't forget that I am from the same neighborhood as you," she plead her case.

"I just didn't think that you were the type," I said while getting the blunts and weed out of my drawer.

"What type is that?" she asked offended.

"You know what I am saying; you are in college, grew up going to a catholic school and all. I just didn't think that you smoked that is all."

"Are you serious? The kids at the catholic schools are even more crooked than the ones in the ghetto; they parents just let them get away with being bad, and even support their habits. Trust me; everything isn't always what it seems. Looks can be deceiving," Charity explained in her proper tone and voice.

"What channel is Lifetime on?" she asked me after turning on my big screen television in my room and positioning her back up against the headboard using both pillows, while also pulling the covers up to her neck.

"I don't know! Do I look like the type of guy who watches Lifetime?" I asked while reaching over to push the menu guide on the remote with one hand and still keeping the partially rolled blunt from spilling the weed with the other.

Without answering my smart question she found the channel she was looking for; then I passed her the lit blunt and went into the kitchen choking on the big well deserved hit I just took to get us both something to drink.

"Do you want something to drink?" I yelled into the room to her the way a married couple would yell still being considerate of their worrisome partners needs.

"What do you got?" she yelled right back, but she used a tone like I was interrupting her show and to leave her alone.

"Everything from Kool-Aid to wine!"

"Wine!" she tried to yell but was stopped by a continuous cough from the hydro weed she was smoking.

"You okay in there?" I asked.

She never answered me so I took that like a yes. I got myself a MGD and put her wine in a Waterford Crystal wine glass that I got hot from one of my stings. We sat back and watched some crazy movie for a while, smoked the blunt and had another drink. The sun had came up before we knew it, and I had completely forgot about sex or the fact that she was almost naked laying next to me. I was enjoying myself with her!

"Do you ever sleep?" she asked me as an invite into my own bed.

"Of course I do," I said while stripping down to my boxers and jumping in bed next to my future wife. "It's just that I usually sleep naked."

Charity was laughing, but still instantly cuddled up under me, and before I could even try anything we were both off into a deep sleep; one of many good nights that we shared doing nothing more than holding each other through the night.

## <u>Chapter 31</u>

"Hello," I said knowing who it was calling me.

"Hey! What is up?" Kelly asked me in a friendly voice.

"Hey," I said feeling relieved that I wasn't at home with Charity when she called.

"What was all of that about last night?" she asked.

"What are you talking about?"

"You know what I am talking about. You hung up on me!"                    .

"Oh, my fault, my phone went dead."

"Well you could've called me back. I was worried about you."

"That is sweet of you," I said in an forgive me voice. "Will you forgive me?"

"I guess so," she said with a giggle. "What time will you be ready for me?"

"UMM, I don't know if I will ever be ready for you," I said playfully. "How about I call you after I get done handling some important business?"

"You better call me back too!" she said and hung up frustrated.

I was on my way to meet up with Stiff at his mother's house so that we could go meet up with Marcus' Mexican connection. Everything had changed overnight for me, and I was now really considering doing something that I had never done before. Charity was still asleep when I left the house, so I decided to not wake her up. Really, I was trying to see what she would do if she woke up in my house and I wasn't there.

"So what did he say on the phone?" I asked Stiff about the connection as he got into my creeper.

"He didn't say anything other than call him when we are ready to meet up at his low rider shop down south," Stiff said.

"Bet, did you tell him that I was coming too?"

"Yeah, he said that he remembered your Escalade truck from when Marcus met up with him in it before."

"What? Don't tell me that that nigga was moving shit in my truck?"

"Naw, he owed the connect some money, and I was with him when he came to the shop before in it."

253

"I ain't tripping on the truck, but I just wouldn't be moving no shit around in nothing flashy like that."

"Shit, I would," Stiff said in a mumble as he rolled up the blunt.

"That is your hot ass!" I laughed.

"You can call it what you like," Stiff giggled.

"I hope you are ready for whatever," I said showing my Colt 45 magnum in the glove box.

"What? Nigga you tripping, I thought you was just playing," Stiff said nervously.

"Don't worry; I plan on copping from him first. Then, we are going to get they asses!"

"Bet, that is what I am talking about anyway," Stiff said excited. "I am ready to take my game to another level."

"Me too! Me too!"

We pulled up to the shop about 15 minutes later both high as a kite off of the hydro. I figured it would be better if I waited in the car for Stiff to go inside first. A few minutes later Stiff and Houlio were both standing in front of the shop waving at me to get out and come inside. At first I didn't notice them; so once I did, I kind of got out in a rush making a fool out of myself.

"This is my guy Tea that I was telling you about," Stiff introduced us.

"What is up?" Houlio said with a nod and a handshake.

"Just chilling!"

"That is cool that you chilling and all, but like I said what is up?" he asked me impatiently.

"Oh, my bad," I told him finally getting the picture. "I was looking to cop something."

"I know that much," he said raising his voice like a boss would speak to a servant. "You ain't the police are you?"

"No, why you ask me some bullshit like that?"

"Just asking, chill out!" he said with a smile realizing that I wasn't feeling his vibe at all. "How much you trying to cop?"

"I want a brick," I said trying to see how he would react.

"How much money do you got?"

"How much are you going to charge me?" I asked ready to just pull my pistol out and make him break bread.

"Look, maybe we got off to a bad start. Let's go inside and finish this conversation," he explained.

Once we got inside I immediately got more relaxed. There were about 10 Mexican's inside working, both men and women. The girls were stitching upholstery, while the guys installed systems. They had it going on.

"Hey Tea!" Houlio called my name loud over the sound of high-powered tools. "Come check this out!"

I followed him into the back area of the shop where they installed the hydraulics and air ride suspension systems at. Then I noticed what he wanted me to see. It was a Chevy Caviler the same year and color as mines, with the same dark tinted windows and all. If it wasn't for the Texas plates and CD player, I would've thought that it was mines.

"You like this car?" he asked me while opening up the passenger side door.

"Not really, why?"

"Why not? This is a good car," he said leaning under the dashboard.

All of a sudden the airbag compartment popped up slowly. I looked again and noticed a small compartment the size of a small carry on suitcase or luggage.

"That is tight!" I said to him still confused.

"Yeah, I kind of figured you would like it."

"Shit, I need you to hook my car up like that!"

"No problem," he said with dollar signs in his eyes. "You can leave it now to get hooked up and drive this one home. It should be finished in a couple of days.

After he got finished showing me his gadgets we went back to the body shop part of the huge building. There was dust everywhere.

"Look at that baby over there," Houlio said pointing at an old 1957 Chevy that was a big hunk of junk. It was all stripped down to the bare metal, it didn't have any wheels or tires on it, the windows were out of the whole car, and the seats were nowhere to be found exposing the holes through the rusted out floor board.

I did not really see what he saw in the car other than the fact that it was a classic.

"What do you mean baby?" I asked laughing under my breath.

"Never judge a book by its cover," he said as he popped the trunk with a screwdriver. "Whola!"

I was totally mesmerized by all of the keys of cocaine and pounds of weed that were inside of the trunk of that car. From estimation, I would have to say that it was at least 50 or so keys of cocaine in that trunk and that the entire stock of weed was obviously hydro.

"Here," Houlio said after handing me one brick and a pound of weed. "You know that Marcus still owes us $10,000?"

"No, I didn't know that."

"Well, if we do business with you, you will have to take on his debt."

"How much do you want for this?" I asked looking at the package that I just received.

"$17,000 for the brick and $3,000 for the trees, so you owe me $20,000," he told me not really caring if I had any money or not on me.

"Well, I got $14,000 on me, so I will bring back the other $6,000 when I pick up my ride. Is that cool?" I asked.

"That's cool but don't ever tell anybody that you fuck with us," he told me.

"Who is us?" I asked curiously.

"You see there are 5 major cocaine distribution families that operate here in the United

States. We happen to belong to the largest one. Every last key that we sell; over 10 people make over $500 off of it, not to mention the many people that make $100. There are even people who make as little a $50 dollars off of every brick sold. Now I know that doesn't sound like a lot of money, but when you consider that we move keys in LA, Denver, West Virginia, Chicago, New York, and here in Indianapolis; well, then you are talking about millions of dollars made throughout the year. We move over a ton a week nation wide, so you can see how wealthy rich we all are. I am only a messenger, so to say, my uncle is the one who gets the cut; but, when he steps down, I will take over his place and get his pension plan," Houlio explained the organized crime family to me.

"Damn that's deep!" I said astonished.

"You know what is even deeper?" he asked me.

"No what?" I asked thirsty for some more game.

"My uncle lives in Mexico and don't even speak any English at all. He hasn't ever seen this place and he owns it."

"That's fucking power," I said.

"No, that is mob shit!"

After Houlio and I wrapped up our little conversation we met back up with Stiff in the front room. He was flirting with a sexy Mexican girl who worked at the front counter.

"You ready?" I asked Stiff with a smile on my face.

"Yeah," Stiff said while writing his cell phone number down for the little chick.

We left the shop in a different car than the one we came in. I had my plates on the back, so it was still the same car if you asked me.

After I dropped Stiff back off at home, I went home to get myself together. I made a promise to hook back up with Stiff, but he never saw any of the dope and weed I had just picked up. He knew something was up though, and was excited to be finally back in the game.

I walked into my house and was immediately caught off guard by Charity: She was laying on the couch, on the phone, and completely naked like she had just gotten out of the shower.

"Oh, here he is now, I will call you back later," Charity told whoever she was on the phone with.

"What is up?" I asked feeling on the spot.

"You tell me what is up. I woke up and you was gone, what is up?" she snapped. "Then I just got up off of the phone with my cousin in South Bend, and she said that you just had a baby. She also said that you and your little girlfriend Candice got robbed by Money last year and that Candice got raped, caught a STD, and got pregnant!"

"That is a new one to me," I said laughing and knowing that she was obviously scared and not used to being involved with anything or anybody like me before.

"Let me finish before you say one word. She told me that you are on the run from the police for killing somebody. Is any of that shit true? Am I going to get into any trouble for messing with you Terry?" she asked me sincerely.

I never answered her question. Really, I couldn't answer her question, because I didn't know what could possibly happen. First thing I did was pulled out and threw the pound of hydro on the table and started to roll up a blunt with Charity staring at me like I was crazy the whole time. Then after a few minutes, I had the blunt rolled up and lit, I passed it to her.

"So, you are not going to answer my questions ha?" she asked me between choking. "Damn, this is some pollutant shit!"

"Yeah, I agree," I said.

"You agree to what?"

"Charity lets get something straight," I snapped. "This is my house that you up in and my couch that you sitting up on naked. As of right now, you don't have any right to ask me shit or talk to anybody about our involvement. If you scared to be around me then we can end this here and now because you haven't lost anything yet; but, if you want to continue fucking with my hot ass, then remember that I make the rules and I break the rules. I don't answer to anybody!"

Charity just sat there dumbfounded for a few moments before even reacting. I could tell that she was taking everything in and deciding in her head if she was willing to sacrifice herself for my bullshit. I am not sure if it was the fact that we didn't have sex the previous night, or the fact that now that she has notified somebody of our involvement made me second guess our chances of a discreet relationship, but I wasn't holding back my tongue at all. She obviously wasn't used to being talked to like that either, because she didn't know how to react. However, if I was to judge from the look she was giving me, I would have to say that she was completely turned on from all of the danger involved with me, and then my tone of voice and cockiness just made her melt. I think that the look of understanding that she gave me made me instantly fall for her too.

"Are you hungry?" I asked her trying to break the tension that was evident in the air. She never answered!

Charity slowly got off of the couch and walked up on me while maintaining the same eye contact and biting her lip at the same time. She then took the blunt out of my hand and put it into the ashtray and gave me the look that will signify sex for years to come.

I took the hint, but before I could do anything she threw one leg up on the love seat that I was sitting on, exposing her beautifully trimmed pussy to my face. All I could do was sit back and let her stand up and straddle my face like it was a Stallion.

She was on her knees on the back of the love seat, riding my face with vengeance. I could barely breathe, my neck was back so far that I almost caught a cramp. Charity loved every minute of her revenge, wanting to see me out of control, showing me that she would always have the final say so in our arguments. She was cursing me out at the top of her lungs, telling me to swallow all of her sweet juices, making me feel so helpless and turned on that I almost came in my pants.

Finally, I picked her up off of my soaking wet face and turned her around. As soon as she landed on the love seat, I pulled out my cock in one fluid motion, trying to get my own revenge for the way she had just treated me by putting it in her mouth. But, she just kept moving her head away, denying me the opportunity to regain control, making me beg for mercy. She never budged.

Eventually, I had gotten tired of trying to get her to let me have my way with her, so I threw all of my clothes off and picked her 125 pound frame up to carry her into my bedroom. After I threw her one the bed, she immediately spread her legs open ready to receive me, but instead I went back to work with my face, loving the special taste of her pussy. It was like none other that I had ever tasted in my life, she had me sprung already!

## The Son of the Streets...
## Terrence leRoy Baker

From the spontaneous way our sex game was playing out, she climaxed within seconds, so I jumped up inside of her welcoming body. She was so wet and excited that I too exploded almost immediately, but still spent enough time to get her to explain to me that the feelings of love were mutual and that she will never leave me no matter what.

Still wanting to get the last word, I pulled out as soon as I felt myself about to cum, and blasted all over her stomach. Charity started hitting me and grabbing at the same time, but not because I came on her, but because I didn't cum inside of her. She pulled until she grabbed my half way soft cock, and put it back inside of her: Then she turned me over and rode me back to hard going for round two. We were both sweaty and all of my cum made a squishy noise in-between our tightly entwined bodies; then out of nowhere came the mother load when her body took over her mind, causing her to shake and almost slip, needing my strength to hold us together. She came uncontrollably!

"You won this war," I said nearly out of breath. "But, I will make sure to see that you never win another one!"

"Oh Yeah! Watch and see!"

"Over my dead body," I said going for the attack and round three.

## Chapter 32

"What is up my nigga?" Tyrone asked after answering the phone. "Long time no see or hear!"

"Just chilling up here in South Bend!"

"You up here?"

"Yeah, you know I just done had another daughter by that young broad Tasha that I was messing with on the low."

"Yeah, I heard about that, but I didn't know that she was pregnant with your baby," Tyrone told me.

"Me either," I told him. "However, everything adds up to when her and a couple of her girls came down to Nap for the Classics Weekend. I was out Cadillac pimpin' and ran into them at the mall. Then, you know the rest was history!"

"Damn my nigga, you need to slow your ass down. What is that 3 kids now?"

"Yeah, something like that!" I said actually realizing that I wasn't worth shit to any of them. "Off of that thought! I need to holla at you about some business."

"Shit I hope you got some good news for your nigga, because the streets is ugly right now. The feds been cracking down tough on everybody, so people laying low with that work, if you know what I mean," Tyrone told me sighing. "Oh yeah, I almost forgot. Red wanted me to get in contact with you for him. It was about a week or so ago. I just blew it off, but he said it was important. He said something about what happened with Money, and that you had to handle your business; some shit like that. He sounded cool, but I didn't trust him enough to even relay his message."

"I will call him later on or something, because it ain't no telling what that nigga want; especially after he just got done doing a small fed bit. You know what I am saying: The feds just don't give out small bits; unless, you on that 5k1 pension plan with them that is!"

"You think the nigga is snitching, or on some set up shit?" Tyrone asked me not too sure if I was serious or just paranoid.

"All I am saying is that you are not getting out of the feds on less than a 5 year bit for cocaine; and not to mention, this nigga done already did state time for work, so you do the math," I told him sternly. "Don't forget that Money was like a son to him either!"

"You are right! I guess I give the nigga too much credit for raising us in the game," Tyrone said feeling dumb.

"Don't be so hard on yourself. Just remember that people change with time and circumstances," I told him like I was teaching him something new. "Be ready to hook up with me in a couple of hours!"

"Cool, just come by the crib or whatever, but call first so I can for sure be at home."

"Holla!"

After I hung up the phone with Tyrone, I went inside of Tasha's house. She lived in an apartment complex, so I was able to sit out in the parking lot for over an hour and simply watch the door and traffic without looking suspicious. I was definitely paranoid at first, but as soon as I saw my beautiful little girl in Tasha's arms at the door, I calmed down instantly.

She was my daughter without a doubt; I knew it from first sight. It was like magic, because as soon as I picked her up into my arms she fell asleep. She knew that she was safe in my arms and that I was her father just as well as I knew she was my daughter. It's funny how the love is already established the moment the seed is planted in the mother's womb, but it is definitely evident.

I didn't say too much; what could I say? Here I am on the run from the feds facing a decade or more in prison, and I have made yet another child that I knew that I could never be a good father to. My life was a reflection of the same carelessness of my own father, and now I am doing what society encourages us all to do: I am following in my father's footsteps. What a shame!

Tasha didn't say much to me either, and unlike with my daughter, the love wasn't there at all between us. She hated my guts; I could see the hate in her eyes. Maybe that was the reason I thought twice before I gave her my cell phone number. She would have control over my freedom once I do, but what the hell! I gave her my number and left without looking back so that she couldn't see the tears welling up in my eyes.

"What it do my nigga?" Tyrone asked me as he gave me a bear hug.

"Man you already know it ain't easy being cheesy! What you done put on some weight or something," I joked, actually he was looking good and in shape.

"No, but did you lose a few hundred pounds?" he asked me seriously. I was stressed out, and stressing and losing weight go hand in hand. "You alright my nigga?"

"Fuck you!" I said embarrassed as I sat down ready to roll up my only temporarily escape from reality. "I am good."

"Something is up with you," he said taking the freshly rolled blunt out of the ashtray to light up and pass to me.

"Yeah, this bunk ass weed you up in here smoking on is what is up!" I choked. "I been done choked to death on one of these seeds!"

"Fuck you!" he said snatching the blunt back from me. "You want a beer?"

"Nigga I don't want one, I need one before I die up in this bitch," I said still choking and laughing at the same time. "Here roll up this real shit!"

"Damn, this is some good shit," he said reaching for the bag. "Hold up, I got some strawberry wraps for this shit."

"That is what I came here to talk about. I got a whole pound of this shit," I told him.

"I don't have any money like that my nigga, especially not for no weed. You know I would smoke a whole pound up in a week."

"Nigga, I ain't trying to sell you no pound of weed. What I was trying to tell your timid ass is that I got this new Mexican connect down in Nap that got everything. These muthafuckas is paid!" I told him excited. "Man when I went to go holla at these crazy muthafuckas at like this rim shop, they had all kinds of shit going on up inside the place. They on some high-tech mob type shit. Then, when this young muthafucka gave me the work out of the back of this old beat down Chevy, it had like 50 or so bricks and 10 or so pounds of this same shit in the trunk of it; and I know it ain't going nowhere anytime soon."

"Damn, you sound like you want to rob these muthafuckas," Tyrone said giving me the blunt to light up.

"Why you say that?"

"Because, you drooling all at the mouth talking about the shit!"

"I might want to rob the muthafuckas. Shit you know how the game is dirty than a bitch. They would rob me if I gave them the chance to."

"Man, be careful fucking with them Mexicans. Ain't no telling what kind of shit they involved in!" Tyrone told me concerned. "What is up with the work though?"

"Oh, yeah, I brought that shit with me."

"Good, because I could probably move that shit pretty fast."

"Well bet, I will leave this brick with you, but don't fuck with it until tomorrow. I am about to sneak over Jasmine's house for the night. If everything is cool, then I will stay over there until tomorrow night."

"That is cool, but be careful my nigga. You already know that is the first place the boys will come looking for you at if they hear that you in town."

"I will be alright!"

## **Chapter 33**

"Who is it?"

"It's me," I told Jasmine through the cracked door.

"Terry?"

"Yeah!" I said frustrated.

"Boy, what are you doing over here this early in the morning," she asked me still not opening up the door. "Come back in about 10 minutes."

Feeling paranoid of some one being in there that I might know, I hurried up and cut up out of there. What was I supposed to do? Even though Jasmine was my baby momma and had love for me, people change with time; I knew that even she couldn't be trusted.

Running out of options, I went straight back over to Tasha's house. Tasha opened the door immediately and then went back to bed without saying a word to me. I just stood there at the doorway in the dark, afraid that anybody could be inside her room with her or with me in this dark unknown room.

"You can come in here! We don't bite," Tasha yelled into the room to me; waking my daughter up at the same time.

"Why don't you put her back to sleep, since you waking everybody up around here?" Tasha sarcastically told me.

"My bad!" I said whispering and attending to my newborn seed.

As soon as I picked her up, she went back to sleep in my arms. Tasha was up on her elbow as if she was waiting for me to mess up or need help, but finally relaxed with a jealous look on her face that lit up the dark room when she noticed that I was no rookie at the parenting game at all.

"I wish you would have been here hours ago, because she has been cutting up all night long. I ain't for this shit!"

"You are doing fine," I told her while I took a seat next to her on the bed. She was very young, only 17 years old, which means probably only 16 when I got her pregnant.

"You don't know shit! It's been over a week and you just now seeing your baby. I should of thought twice about fucking with your no good ass!" Tasha snapped changing the vibe and warm mood intentionally. I could tell that she had feelings for me, and that she didn't even understand why.

"I am sorry that life is so fucked up, but please lower your voice before you wake up my baby!" I said.

"Your baby! UMM."

The whole night we went back and forth that way. She would snap at me, and I would accept her cursing. Before you knew it, we were waking up holding each other. Tasha was every small and petite, so that and the fact that she was young always turned me on. She didn't hate me, it just took time to get everything off of her chest for her to realize that I wasn't as bad of a person as it seemed. Besides, once we had a child together, we became family.

"I though that I told you to come back in a minute or two," Jasmine said to me as soon as I answered my phone the next morning.

"Girl please, I ain't about to be playing around like that. I got too much to lose!"

"Where are you at?" she asked me jealously. "Are you still in town?"

"Yeah, why?"

"Can you meet me at my house? I am about to go on my lunch break," she asked me obviously wanting some midday sex. I was once too on her lunch break sex schedule, so I too could use some good loving.

"You know I don't make any moves around here in the daytime."

"Boy ain't nobody thinking about your ass. Where are you at? Over Candice's house I bet," she was saying as I hung up on her before she trapped me into her web.

I was already laid up with Tasha, and even though we didn't have sex the night before, I knew that I could get some if I pressed the issue. She was already in the shower and ready for some fun and games. The only thing that stopped me the previous night was the fact that it hasn't yet been 4 weeks for her to heal up, which honestly, I really didn't give a fuck about anyway. There were all sorts of other ways for me to get off.

Instead I called my nigga to get my mind off of my early morning bullshit.

"Damn nigga, I been calling your ass all morning! You had me worried," Tyrone told me. "I got like five people lined up to buy bricks, so what is up?"

"Shit, go ahead and sell that muthafucka then. I am ready to get the fuck out of here," I told him. Tasha was listening in while drying off her naked body on the edge of the bed. She was offended!

"Man, I got rid of that last night," Tyrone told me. "You need to go get something else."

"You did?" I asked knowing already that he would dip into the brick when I left it in the first place. Shit the only reason I didn't want him to mess with it was because I wanted to sell it whole, so I knocked down two birds with one brick. "That is cool; I will be over your house as soon as it gets dark."

"Bet, just call first my nigga."

"One."

"Fuck you Tea!" Tasha snapped. "You ain't shit! I can't believe you!"

"Girl what is you tripping on now?"

"You don't won't to be here then get the fuck out!" she went off waking my daughter up again.

"Stop tripping, I want to be here," I said wrapping my arms around her. She acted like she didn't want me to touch her for all of one second, then fell back into me and laid there. Tears were in her eyes, but she was one of the strongest women I had ever messed with; she wouldn't let them fall.

"I just wish shit didn't have to be this way," she told me sadly.

"Trust me, I do too," I told her as I covered her naked body up into the covers next to me. My daughter was on the bed next to us and fell back to sleep after being simply touched and comforted.

We all just laid there in silence for a while before falling asleep. All I could think about was how many families I had started. So many times have I laid up with the mother and my child like life was a joke. How could I ever have something real and solid? My children all deserved a better life than the one I could ever offer them. I needed to get me some money, so that I can at least try to make a difference. This lifestyle just isn't the way I want to live. I needed to make some drastic changes in my moral values, because my children need to be more of a priority.

"How much is here?" I asked Tyrone after he handed me the grocery bag full of money.

"$23, 000," he told me hesitantly. "I didn't know what you wanted for it, but you know you are my guy, and I can tell shit isn't going too good right now for you. So, just give me whatever you can afford. Really, you need to just come right back with some more work. That shit went quick!"

"That shouldn't be a problem, but I don't want to be driving up here every other day. I need to get the mother load!"

"There you go again," he said.

"What do you mean?"

"My nigga, don't go out there and do nothing stupid."

"Look, I know what I am doing, but what I need you to do is be ready if I call you," I told him.

"You know I am always ready, but I ain't on no robbery shit."

"Shut your scary ass up! I don't need you to do anything but make a big order on the phone so that the connect can hear you and he may trust me with a bigger load."

"Oh, I can do that!"

"Still, I am going to take his shit! I am getting too old for all of this hustling and shit. It is time for me to settle down."

"Where did all of this come from? You settling down? Yeah right!" Tyrone laughed at me. "With who?"

"You wouldn't believe me if I told you."

"Who my nigga?"

"Do you remember that girl Charity that I told you I was going to marry back when we were only pups in the game?"

"Yeah, what about her!"

"That is my girl my nigga," I confidently told him. "And she got her shit together too. She is in college and maintaining a 4.0; she looks good as hell; she obviously has feelings for me; and plus, it has to be meant to be for us to run into each other like we did. What we have is like nothing I have ever experienced with any other woman before."

"Nigga you said that shit before about the last bitch that told on your ass and got you in this shit you in now!"

"Stop lying! You know I ain't never told you no shit like that about any women before. All of the other women that I was serious about was for different reasons, but this one is because I really want to be with and around her. We can just kick it without no sex or nothing. Man she is cool as hell!"

"Yeah, but just don't go and mess her life up like you did all of the other women you messed up before deciding that it wasn't right in the first place."

"Oh that is cold!" I told Tyrone with my feelings crushed. "Man I was young then, but now I am looking at life from a whole other level. I want to spend the rest of my life with somebody now."

"Do you mean the rest of your freedom?" Tyrone asked me bringing me back to reality. "What do you think will happen if and when you get caught up with? Do you think that she will still be in your corner when you doing years in prison?"

"She said that she would never leave me no matter what!" I said sounding lame and blinded by love.

"Nigga, don't be stupid. Charity is the baddest bitch that came from this North Side, if not the baddest bitch that done come from this city.

*The Son of the Streets...*
*Terrence leRoy Baker*

Good, fine, intelligent, and did I say fine. Women like that just don't wait on niggas who go to prison. You got to find you a fat white girl for that," he told me coldly.

"Why are you hating on me?"

"Hating? I would never do anything like that. I love you my nigga! I just don't want you to get sidetracked and lose focus. You know how weak your ass is when it comes to women. Shit, now that you done told me all of this, now I understand why you are even considering robbing them Mexicans. You would never be talking like this if you didn't have something or somebody you trying to impress with a bunch of bullshit. You need to be focused on your freedom; don't make focusing on your life complicate things even more than they already are."

Tyrone was simply being brutally honest with me, and you know what? He was right! I would never even let the thought about robbing somebody cross my mind, but I wasn't doing it for Charity, I was doing it for myself. It is hard out in these evil streets, and all I need is one good run in the game to make enough money to get out of it, maybe open up some legal businesses or buy up some real-estate. First thing I needed to do was talk to Charity about everything except for the lick.

"Look my nigga!" I told Tyrone after a few moments of silence. "Be ready when I call you!"

"I will!" he told me disappointed.

279

## <u>Chapter 34</u>

"Stiff?" I yelled into the phone receiver.

"What is up my nigga?" Stiff asked me waking up out of his sleep.

"You ready?"

"Not really, but I got some money for you if you need it," Stiff told me finally getting up.

"Look, I need to come holla at you about something. Call the Essay and tell him that we need to hook up with him," I told him. "I will be over there as soon as I get off of the highway.

I didn't really want to tell Stiff what it was that I wanted to do over the phone. I knew that he would be ready to ride out for the cause, so I just went to pick him up. But first, I had to make a detour to my house to grab my pistol. Who knew what to expect?

"What is up?" Stiff asked me worried about my urgency.

"I think it is about time to hit that lick on the Mexicans," I told him after pulling away from his curb.

"Are you serious?"

"Hell yeah, I am serious!" I snapped looking at him instead of keeping my eyes on the road. "You ain't scared are you?"

"No, but I thought you were just bullshitting," he told me. "Roll up something, shit I need to get the jitters out of me first."

"Don't get too nervous because we may not even have to pull out the pistol. I have a plan," I told him passing the pre-rolled blunt out of the ashtray to him.

"Oh yeah, well what is the plan?"

"You see, I am going to tell him that I got somebody up in South Bend that wants to order something big, something like 10 or 20 bricks. Then I am going to have him talk to my guy on the phone who is already laced up, and he will tell him that he won't buy the bricks unless he gets the price he wants, which is $15,000 a piece just to make the story authentic. I already know that they going to say that they will go no lower than $16,000 a brick. However, once they see how serious the story adds up, then they will have no choice to say yea or nay. Now if they take me back there where the bricks are at again, and I see a load like I did last time, then I will use the pistol to hold them up while you load up my car, that is conveniently already up at the shop," I told him confident that my plan was flawless.

"Fuck it, I am ready for whatever! It ain't nothing to it but to do it, then we can worry about the consequences later," Stiff told me hyping himself up. What he didn't know was that I was just as nervous as he was.

We pulled up at the shop and just like I planned. My car wasn't out front, which meant only one thing, it was inside where it needed to be. It was early in the morning, so the shop was pretty much empty, except for a new Mexican named Paco and the same girl that Stiff talked to last time we showed up. I had forgotten all about her, and was worried that she may have hooked up with Stiff, but what the hell. That wasn't my problem to deal with. I was on one mission, and that was to get this cheddar.

"What is up amigo's?" Paco asked as if he had done business with us several times before.

"Where is Houlio?" I asked knowing that Paco was one of those knucklehead muthafuckas that I would possibly have to put a hole in.

"Oh, Houlio is out of town on business, but he sends his regards," he told me with a mischievous smile like Houlio just didn't make the cut and would never be seen again. Paco was a straight up killer and for a minute I was scared he might have the same plans for us that we had for him. "So you got the money, here is your package."

"Yeah, I got your money, but there is something else I need to holla at you about," I told him grabbing the book bag with one brick and another pound of weed in it. These Mexicans had they shit tight!

"What is up?" he asked me suspiciously.

"I got a guy up in South Bend that wanted to grab some serious weight," I said sounding like I was on some bullshit. He looked straight through me too.

"What do you mean he wants to grab some serious weight," Paco said making a slight retreat back.

"Hold the fuck up!" I said pulling out my pistol and pointing it at his head. "Don't make me pull this trigger!"

"It's cool, just don't do nothing stupid," he said loud enough for the girl at the front desk to hear us and the commotion.

"Oh my God! What are you doing?" She screamed at the top of her lungs.

POP! POP! Was all you could hear; I blew her heart out of her back from reflexes. She still had her mouth open as she fell to the ground. The whole room went silent; even I couldn't realize how far things were going so fast.

"Homes! Homes! Don't shoot!" Paco said putting his hands high over his head.

"Chill out! Come on," I told him motioning for us to make our way back into the area where the old Chevy was at. I gave Stiff a look like I didn't want things to happen the way they were. He just stood nervously, still shaking his head.

"Okay, I will give you all of the money and dope, just please let me live," Paco told me falling to the ground to open the trunk of the car. "I knew you niggers couldn't be trusted."

He opened up the trunk and just as I expected it was loaded. There was even more dope and weed than last time. Stiff immediately straightened himself out once he saw the quantity of merchandise. He went straight to my creeper that was in the same room; he popped the trunk on my car and went to work.

"Paco, I am going to ask you this one time. Where is the money?"

"What money?" he asked me. "There is no money."

POP! I sent one single shot through the back of his head blowing blood and brains all over the dope and weed in the trunk of the car. Stiff finished moving the dope into my creeper; I went to get the girls body to put into the trunk of the Chevy once we got everything together and loaded into my car.

"What are you doing?" Stiff asked me noticing that I was getting an old mop bucket full of dirty water. "We need to go!"

284

"Calm down my nigga! Help me put these bodies in this trunk, and then after we mop up the blood in both of these rooms, we going to set this place on fire."

"Hurry up!" Stiff yelled getting my point and grabbing a can of gasoline that was in the corner. He then started to pour gas all over the bodies inside of the trunk. Momentarily, we were leaving behind a murder scene full of smoke.

"Whoa! My nigga we pulled it off," Stiff was yelling hyped up and scared at the same time.

"Calm down my nigga, calm down, the police are right behind us," I told him looking in the rear view mirror.

"Oh shit!" Stiff said turning completely around to look out of the back window.

The police instantly turned on their sirens. We both got nervous because the car was sagging in the back from all of the weight in the truck. Luckily for us, the cop car did a u-turn and went into the opposite direction towards the scene of the crime that we left behind us.

"Man you need to chill!" I told Stiff.

"You right, that could have been our asses," Stiff was saying while also looking into the purse that was on the floor. "Who is Charity?"

"Oh, that's this girl that I mess with."

"She fine! You need to wife her, she in college," he said noticing that her ID was a Purdue ID.

"After we sit down and see how much work we got, maybe I will wife her. Shit, I might even go buy her a brand-new Lexus or something," I said feeling myself and trying to realize how much money we just hit for.

We got over to my house and found out that we had took 60 bricks of cocaine and 12 pounds of hydro. The numbers didn't even add up to me, but I did know that we were rich. Stiff only got 15 bricks and 3 pounds of weed, which was about 25% of the whole lick. In all actuality that was fair, considering the fact that I planned everything out and killed two people. I was really all messed up behind the fact that I had killed them so easily; it was like nothing to me. I think Stiff was happy with whatever he got, because he was still obviously nervous that I may turn my pistol and kill him too. I may be grimy, but not that grimy!

The very next day like a fool, I went back up to Golden Rule Auto and put the $20,000 thousand that I ended up keeping down on a black 2002 S500 AMG kitted Mercedes. They charged me $50,000 for it, but told me that if I could pay it off in the first thirty days, that they would give it to me for $45,000. Just like before I took it straight up to Mobile Jams to my guy Mike Rudy. He hooked me up with some 20inch Lowenhart rims, with a 20 by

9 in the front and a 20 by 10 in the back off set. I
was stunting.

Stiff was with me and bought him an all
black 2003 745i BMW, and put some Street Davin
spinning rims on it. His credit wasn't as good as
mine with Golden Rule, so instead, he paid $40,000
cash for the car and another $10,000 for the rims
from Mobile Jams. Stiff knew everybody in the city,
so as soon as he touched his bricks, he was selling
them like they were cheeseburgers out of Mc
Donald's. I knew that he wouldn't make it a good
year at the rate he was splurging, but couldn't blame
him, I was the same young fool before too.

I still was sitting on my whole batch of
bricks, and knew that from Stiff's actions that I
needed to move quickly before he and his crew of
niggas be in my house with a pistol to my head. The
game was just cold like that.

Shortly after getting my car, I found me a
nice condo outside of the city up in Giest on the
Reservoir. It was a 3000 square feet tri-level condo:
with all white carpets; glass walls that could only be
seen out of; fireplaces in every room, including the
dining room; and marble floors throughout the
whole estate. There was a security guard that
patrolled the grounds; you needed a pass just to
visit. I was living grand, and for the $2,500 a month
they charged me, it was worth every penny.

## **Chapter 35**

"Hey baby," Charity told me with a seductive accent coming into my new establishment. "This place is nice!"

"Thank you! It is all yours," I told her throwing the set of keys that I had put to the side for her. Intentionally, I didn't explain to her that an extra key to my Benz was also included.

"Stop playing," she said looking at the keys and paying close attention to the little black box with the Mercedes symbol on it. The condo had an attached garage, so she didn't see anything coming in; still, she just left it alone and made herself at home. "Who decorated this place?"

"I paid an interior design agency to lay it out for me."

"Nigga, what you done did, hit the lottery or something?" she asked me knowing that everything just wasn't adding up. "What do you got going on? Either you done hit the lotto or robbed a bank; what you been up to?"

"Nothing," I lied knowing that she didn't care one way or another. "Let's go shopping?"

"What is going on Terry?"

"Nothing! Would you chill out?"

"Okay, but don't be having me on no bullshit with you," she told me excited and nervous at the same time. "Where we going shopping at?"

"Chicago," I said nonchalantly.

"Chicago?" she asked.

"Yeah, and you driving. But, first, we need to make a detour up to South Bend," I told her.

"South Bend? For what?"

"Why are you asking me all of these questions all of a sudden?" I asked feeling her untrustworthy vibe. "What, you don't trust me?"

"No."

"Good."

We waited until it was dark outside to hit the highway in my new Mercedes. I had 10 bricks inside the trunk of the car that Charity didn't know anything about. I just figured why worry her to death like that; besides, I never really officially told her that I sold drugs for a living. Of course she knew though.

Charity loved the car; she drove it like a true queen should. The whole ride I couldn't help but to admire at how good she fit in the driver's seat of my car. Still, I wouldn't roll up any weed and was constantly telling her about her speed, which was hard to control in a car that drove so smooth.

Instead of making my usual rounds, we went over to her mother's house, who I haven't seen in decades, but still knew exactly who I was. Charity must have been telling her about us, because her mother already knew that I was on the run from the police, which didn't surprise me because every once in awhile they would broadcast my face on the news or in the paper. Still, her mother was very nice to me.

"Damn my nigga!" Tyrone said after getting out of his car in front of Charity's mother's house. "You didn't tell me that you were driving in a big boy Benz, I thought you done went and bought you a girly car or something."

"Fuck you!" I told him feeling comfortable outside in the open only because it was late and I wasn't in familiar territory. "Here!"

"What in the fuck am I supposed to do with all of this?" Tyrone asked me looking inside of the suitcase that was full of bricks and weed.

"Nigga, what the fuck do you mean what are you supposed to do with it?"

"I am just saying. What is in here?" he asked me while taking out the massive load from the trunk.

"Just know that you owe me $210,000."

"What! You trying to get me killed nigga?" Tyrone asked me excited. "You must have really pulled off that shit?"

"Yeah, I did."

"Well don't even trip my nigga. As soon as I get this shit safely home, I will holla back at you. O wants me to let him know when I touch back down. He said save him a brick, so I will bring that money back to you in a couple of hours."

"Take your time my nigga. I don't want you running around like no fool; a nigga will peel your cap back over this shit," I told my ace boon coon.

"Man chill out! You the only nigga that I need to watch," he joked seriously. "With your grimy ass!"

"That's for us?" I asked with my feelings hurt. "You ain't right."

"You know you still my favorite horse even if you never win another race," Tyrone said getting in his car to leave. I stuck my middle finger up at him as he pulled off.

After hooking up with Tyrone, Charity and I took the toll road out to Chicago. It was after midnight when we got there, so instead of going straight to our room at the Peninsula downtown, we went out to have a drink and discuss our future together.

"Hey, Charity?" I said after taking a gulp of my Top shelf Margarita.

"What is up?" she asked me enjoying herself and every moment that we have spent together so far.

"Will you marry me?"

"What?" she asked me almost choking on her mimosa. "You better have a ring in your hand the next time you ask me some shit like that."

"The last time I asked you, you said no," I reminded her of our childhood.

"Maybe if you would've had a ring in your hand then things would have been different," we both laughed and left things like that. I had a plan, and she didn't have a clue how serious I really was.

That next morning I made a trip to Tiffany and Co to cop her an 8 carat monster: it was on a platinum band and had two 1.5 cart matching princess cut diamonds surrounding a 5 cart emerald shape diamond in the middle, all vvs cut. I also purchased her a platinum rope and put a 3 cart vvs cut heart shaped medallion to match the 3 cart heart shaped medallion on her bracelet. I spent a total of $35,000 icing her completely out.

After I got back to the room, I hurried up and placed the boxes of jewelry under the towels on the ledge of the Jacuzzi which sat in a room by itself. Then I sneaked back into the bedroom where Charity was still sleep. I eased inside of the bed next to her and then slowly started to kiss all over her back to let her know that I was up and ready to go. She was still hung over from the drinks and bottles of wine we shared the previous night, but still eased back into me to show me that she felt my presence.

As I slowly rubbed her back, she pushed her naked behind up into my already aroused dick, giving me the go ahead to enter into her early morning sexual paradise. I took her invite and while still on my side, slid inside of her slow and passionately.

I don't know if it was the $35,000 that I had just spent on her that she was still unaware of, or her welcoming body, but I was horny, excited, and came within seconds.

Still, I wasn't going to let anything like that stop me from pleasing my woman, so I aggressively got on top of her, maintaining my erection and made love to her for the next hour or so non-stop. Charity fully awoke now and mutually aroused, took over for the last showdown, determined not to be out don. First she straddled me, and then she humped up and down on me long stroking me with a fierce rhythmic flow. She had me screaming to her telling her how much I loved her, but once she knew she was about to make me explode, she jumped up one last time and off of me.

Sitting up and frustrated I gave her a look that was both begging and demanding that she finished what she started, so she slowly crawled to the ledge of the bed with her back to me exposing her dripping wet pussy to my hungry eyes. I jumped up at the notion, and walked around the bed, turning her around and entering into her warm wet pussy from behind while she was on the bed on her knees and I was standing up on the side of the bed, giving me direct access to her body and full control.

Sweaty and tired I pounded away at her holding on to her hips not giving her the luxury of an escape. With every stroke that I gave her, her pussy gave me a gushing amount of cum onto the top of my rock hard dick. The sight was amusing, but the sound of her moans was the most beautiful sound that I had ever heard in my life.

After I couldn't take anymore, I laid down on top of her back still inside of her and finished the job, cumming inside of her as I continued to pound away.

"So, now that you done said you will marry me, what will you do if I get caught by the police?" I asked her feeling like I may have just wasted a bankroll. We were laying back in the Jacuzzi with candles all around us.

"Boy, stop asking me silly questions like that! I told you that I will never leave you, so if you go to prison, then I will go back to school and get my masters degree or PHD depending on how long you have to do, but I promise you that I will wait for you."

"I don't know why, but I do believe you. Anyways, when will you take your finals?" I asked her while purposely knocking over the towels on the ledge.

"You don't pay any attention to me at all. I already took my finals last week. All I am waiting for is graduation," she was saying while also trying to catch the towels before they get soaked by the water that has made its way from the tub to the floor. "Oh, my god, what is this?"

"What?" I asked trying to not spoil the surprise and looking over her shoulder. "Will you marry me?"

"Yes," she speechlessly said still not having opened up the boxes yet. All she knew was that they came from Tiffany's. "How? Where? When?"

"Shhhhh. Just tell me if you can move in with me immediately so that we can be together starting now on," I said stopping her in mid sentence with a passionate kiss.

"Boy you are so slow, that was the plan way before I even came up to Indianapolis and so happened to walk off into paradise; Now this!" Charity told me referring to our new condo and her box full of ice that she just opened up and couldn't even speak on. "I just can't believe it's real, and still don't know what the hell you done been up to."

"Don't start that shit again," I said while tickling her under the water.

"On the way home, I need to stop in West Lafayette to grab all of my things. Is that cool with you?" she asked while immediately putting on her massive ring. Then she turned around to sit on my lap so that she could get me inside of her turned on body as soon as possible.

"You're the one driving," I whispered to her while she was fondling around in the water with my growing cock, trying to put it inside of her soft, hard, or anyway that she could. They were right when they said that diamonds are girl's best friend, because they made Charity go wild.

We pulled up in front of her old apartment in West Lafayette to get her belongings. Everything was going perfect for me. I had finally solidified my life with the woman of my dreams. Actually walking down that isle wasn't as important as hearing her say that she would marry me. I was happy for the very first time in my life and felt complete.

Tyrone always told me that women would be the death of me, and he also said that I would lose focus as soon as I took Charity too serious. Well, even though he was right, good love like the kind that I was feeling was worth dying over.

Holding each other we walked up to her building without a care in the world. I wasn't looking over my shoulder anymore or in the rear view mirror, all I was doing was looking into the eyes of my future wife.

As she put her house key that was on her new key chain into the door, she looked over her shoulder at me to give me that beautiful smile of hers. Only, that smile instantly turned into a paranoiac frown when she realized that it wasn't only me behind her.

I didn't even have time to react to the frantic look in her eyes or even understand before it was too late. She took the first bullet into her arm before falling into mines, where she took another one in her shoulder through my back.

At first I still didn't realize that it was really happening, I had no idea that I was shot, all I knew was that my wife was on the ground before me taking bullets that were meant for me. Simultaneously after I realized what was happening, I turned around to face our attackers, but after I got a good look at him, even the surprise on my face at who it was couldn't change the fact that he was still pulling the trigger. I took three more shots: one in my stomach; one in my arm; and another one into my chest.

All I could hear was the constant clicking of the pistol signaling that the revolver was empty that he was shooting with. I was now completely covering Charity's body, but didn't have anyway of knowing if she was alive under me or not, everything just faded away.

Even after I heard several noises over my body, I couldn't distinguish any of them or understand. I could hear everything but couldn't open my eyes. I heard my newborn daughter, my son, my oldest daughter, Charity's mother, my mother, and even an airplane going over my head, but for some reason, I couldn't hear the only voice that mattered the most, Charity's.

I knew that I was dead, and selfishly, I was hoping that I would be able to see Charity again in the after life: she had so much promise. Was there such a thing as reincarnation? Will she get a second chance? Will I get a second chance?

I had so many questions that will go unanswered, and was leaving so much behind, yet taking so much with me. Who would've ever thought that that decision that I made so many years ago would have an outcome like this. Is it really over!?

The saying goes if you live by the sword, you die by the sword. I guess the sword in my life was the streets.

# Epilogue

I know, I know you all want to know what happened and why it ended the way it did, but just realize that this is the way the streets really are. There are so many murders where only the victims know who it was that actually pulled the trigger, and the murderer could be the very same person that carries the casket at the funeral. The truth of the matter is that the person who killed them is not important, because there will be plenty of Tea's to take his place, as well as many more innocent Charity's to take the bullets that weren't meant for them, simply because they chose to get involved with the wrong type of man.

This story is a basic example of the effect that we all as parents (whether already or in the future) can have on our children. Just think of how many lives this one bad seed affected, and how his children will now grow up without even having the option of knowing who their father was and why he died. Then, look at the fact that Charity could never even have that opportunity to have a family of her own.

There is going to be a lot of people out there who will say, "well I was raised by a single mother and I made it," but those are the people who's stories get told. But, what about the thousands of us who will never get that opportunity to tell our story; or the many who didn't even have the luxury of that single mother who stood by our sides through the thick and the thin. Some of the many children who are raised in these single family homes end up losing that too, and then they are left to be raised by the streets. We are the product of the streets, and that abandonment we experienced is the reason why we never think about the consequences of our actions before we go out there and make these babies that we know we will never be able to provide that home for; the reason why we are so quick to chose to make the dope game a career instead of a habit; and we all look at STD's like it is a normal thing to go through.

As father's we have to start caring about teaching our children about the birds and the bees, about STD's, about the value of family, and most of all, that we love them. As mother's we have to stop thinking about ourselves and our future over the future of the children that we may be left to take care of alone. I know how hard it is to face, but some of the time, you as mother's are the only hope that even us as men have left. So when we lose that for whatever reason, then we lose the only hope that we have left for a better life, and stop caring what happens to us or how we live or die.